"What are we g... **came out and asked. "What are** *you* **going to do?" she amended.**

He didn't ask her to clarify, but he did look as if he wanted to repeat the question to her. "I wish there was an easy fix for this."

So did she. But there wasn't, and it was breaking her heart. Cameron must have seen that as well, because he said some profanity under his breath and pulled her to him. Lauren didn't resist. Nor did she stop herself from looking up at him. It was a mistake, of course, because they were already too close to each other. Especially their mouths. And that was never a good thing when it came to Cameron and her.

"I should go back into the kitchen," he said.

But he didn't, and Lauren didn't let go of him, either, so he could. Instead, she slipped her arm around his waist, drawing him even closer than he already was.

It was almost too much, and in some ways, it wasn't nearly enough.

Because it made her want more of him.

LAWMAN FROM HER PAST

USA TODAY Bestselling Author

DELORES FOSSEN

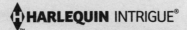
HARLEQUIN INTRIGUE®

Recycling programs
for this product may
not exist in your area.

ISBN-13: 978-1-335-52622-9

Lawman from Her Past

Copyright © 2018 by Delores Fossen

Printed in U.S.A.

www.Harlequin.com

Delores Fossen, a *USA TODAY* bestselling author, has sold over fifty novels, with millions of copies of her books in print worldwide. She's received a Booksellers' Best Award and an RT Reviewers' Choice Best Book Award. She was also a finalist for a prestigious RITA® Award. You can contact the author through her website at www.deloresfossen.com.

Books by Delores Fossen

Harlequin Intrigue

Blue River Ranch

Always a Lawman
Gunfire on the Ranch
Lawman from Her Past

The Lawmen of Silver Creek Ranch

Grayson
Dade
Nate
Kade
Gage
Mason
Josh
Sawyer
Landon
Holden

HQN Books

A Wrangler's Creek Novel

Lone Star Cowboy
(ebook novella)
Those Texas Nights
One Good Cowboy
(ebook novella)
No Getting Over a Cowboy
Just Like a Cowboy
(ebook novella)
Branded as Trouble
Cowboy Dreaming
(ebook novella)

Visit the Author Profile page at Harlequin.com.

CAST OF CHARACTERS

Deputy Cameron Doran—When this tough Texas lawman learns his nephew might have been switched at birth, it puts him and the baby in the crosshairs of a killer.

Lauren Beckett—She left her family's Texas ranch after her parents were murdered ten years ago. To protect her son, she returns home and puts his safety and hers in the hands of the lawman she left behind.

Patrick Lange—The son Lauren had with her late husband, Alden. When Alden died, Patrick became co-owner of his father's wealthy estate, and that could be a motive for a killer.

Isaac Doran—The toddler Cameron has been raising. Cameron loves the boy as his own and has no plans to give him up, even if there has been a baby switch.

Gilly Doran—Cameron's late sister, who died shortly after childbirth. Her dying wish was that Cameron would protect her son from the infant's abusive father, Trace Waters, and Gilly's domineering mother, Evelyn.

Evelyn Waters—She believes she has the right to raise her grandson and thinks Gilly switched the babies at birth to prevent her from doing that.

Julia Lange—Alden's sister resents that his infant son inherited the bulk of his estate. But would she kill Lauren and her brother's child to get her hands on the money?

Duane Tulley—A businessman who's filed a lawsuit against Lauren to get control of the company he co-owned with her late husband. There's enough bad blood between Lauren and him to be motive for murder.

Chapter One

Someone was watching him. Deputy Cameron Doran was certain of it.

He slid his hand over the gun in his waist holster and hoped he was wrong about the bad feeling that was snaking down his spine. Hoped he was wrong about the being watched part, too.

But he knew he wasn't.

He'd worn a badge for eleven years, and paying attention to that bad feeling had saved him a time or two.

With his gun ready to draw, Cameron glanced around his backyard. Such that it was. Since his house was on the backside of the sprawling Blue River Ranch, his yard was just a smear of grass with the thick woods only about fifteen feet away. There were plenty of trees and underbrush. The edge of the river, as well. However, there were also trails that someone could use to make their way to his house.

Someone like a killer.

You'll all die soon.

That was what the latest threatening letter had said. The one that Cameron had gotten just two days ago. Not exactly words anyone wanted to read when they opened their mail, but he'd gotten so many now that they no longer held the emotional punch of the first one he'd gotten a couple of months ago. Still, he wasn't about to dismiss it.

Cameron had another look around, trying to pick through the thick clusters of trees, but when he didn't see anyone, he finished off his morning coffee and went inside. Normally, he would have made a beeline to the nursery so he could say goodbye to his nephew, Isaac, before heading off to work at the Blue River Sheriff's Office, but this morning he went to the window over the sink and kept watch.

From the other side of the house, he could hear Isaac fussing, probably because the nanny, Merilee, was changing his diaper. Isaac was only a year old, but he got up raring to go. He objected to the couple of minutes delay that the diapering caused.

Just when Cameron was about to decide that the bad feeling had been wrong after all, he saw it. Someone moving around. Since those particular trees butted right up against an old ranch trail, the movement got his complete attention.

"Merilee," he called out to the nanny. "Keep Isaac in the nursery a little while longer. And stay away from the windows."

Cameron knew it would alarm the woman, but there was nothing he could do about that now. If this turned out to be a false alarm, then he could smooth things over with her. But for now, Isaac's and her safety had to come first.

He drew his gun, and as soon as he opened the door a couple of inches, Cameron spotted more movement. And the person who was doing the moving.

A woman peered out from one of the trees, and even though she was still pretty far from him, he caught a good enough glimpse of her face.

Lauren Beckett.

She stepped out in full view of him so he got an even better look. Yeah, it was Lauren, all right. She still had the same brunette hair that she'd pulled back into a ponytail. The same willowy build. The last time he'd seen her she'd been a teenager, barely eighteen, but the years hadn't changed her much.

If he'd ventured a guess of who might have been lurking around his place, he would have never figured it would be her. Especially since he'd built his house on Beckett land. *Her* family's land. Of course, Lauren hadn't considered her siblings actually family— or him a friend—in nearly a decade.

Cameron felt the punch of old emotions. Ones he didn't want to feel. He and Lauren had parted ways long ago, and he hated that the tug in his body was still there for her.

He looked at her hands. At her wedding ring. She was still wearing it though he knew her husband had died from cancer a year and a half ago when Lauren had been pregnant. Of course, she might still be wearing the ring because she and her late husband had a child together. A son, if he remembered correctly.

Who was he kidding? He remembered, all right. Little details about Lauren just stuck in his head whether he wanted them there or not.

"What are you doing back there?" he asked.

He started to reholster his gun but then stopped when she fired glances all around her. Lauren had her teeth clamped over her bottom lip, and she motioned for him to come to her.

Hell.

He'd been right about that bad feeling. Something was wrong.

"What happened?" he demanded, but she just kept motioning.

Cursing under his breath, Cameron stepped out and locked the door behind him. Judging from Lauren's nervous gestures, someone else could be out there, and he didn't want that person getting into the house. Keeping watch around him, Cameron gripped his gun with two hands and started toward her.

More memories and emotions came. It'd been ten years since he had seen her. Since he'd kissed her. Ten years since their worlds had turned on a dime. Her mother and father had been murdered. Butchered, really, and even though their killer had been convicted and was behind bars, Lauren hadn't thought justice had been fully served.

Because she also blamed Cameron for not doing enough to save her folks.

That was okay because Cameron blamed himself, too.

All of those thoughts vanished for a moment, though, when he made it to her and stopped about two feet away. Still close enough to catch her scent and see those intense blue eyes. She didn't say anything. Lauren just stood there, staring at him, but he could tell from the tight muscles in her face that this wasn't a social visit.

Not that he thought it would be.

No. Lauren had said her final goodbye to him a decade ago, so it must have taken something pretty bad to come to him this way. Unless…maybe she wasn't here for him.

"Your brothers probably haven't left for work yet and are still home," he told her. They didn't live far, either. "Gabriel lives in his old place, and Jameson has a cabin about a half mile from here."

She didn't seem the least bit surprised about that, which meant maybe Lauren had kept up with her family, after all. Good. Because Cameron wasn't the only one who thought of Lauren often. So did her brothers and her sister, Ivy.

"I can't go to them." Her voice was raw and strained.

"Because you broke off ties with them," Cameron commented. "Don't worry about that. You're still their sister, and they'll help you. They love you," he added, hoping that would ease the tension he could practically feel radiating off her.

Lauren blinked, shook her head. "No. Because their houses are on the main road and someone might see me." She turned, glancing around again, and that was when Cameron spotted the gun tucked in the back waist of her jeans.

He cursed again. "What's wrong?"

A weary sigh left her mouth. The kind of reaction a person had when there was so much wrong that she didn't know where to start. But Cameron figured he knew what this was about.

"We've all been getting threatening letters and emails," he volunteered. "I'm guessing you got one, too?"

She nodded and dismissed it with a shake of her head. "You're raising your sister's child?"

Again, she'd managed to stun him. First with her arrival and now with the question. It didn't seem the right thing to ask since this wasn't a "catching up" kind of conversation.

"Gilly's son, Isaac," Cameron clarified. It had been a year since his kid sister's death, and he still couldn't say her name without it feeling as if someone had put a meaty fist around his heart. "What about him?"

Lauren didn't jump to answer that. With her forehead bunched up, she glanced behind her again. "Is he...okay?"

Isaac was fine. Better than fine, actually. His nephew

was healthy and happy. That wasn't what he said to Lauren, though. "Why are you asking?"

"I need to see him. I need to see Gilly's son."

That definitely wasn't an answer.

Cameron didn't bother cursing again, but he did give her a flat look. "I'll want to know a lot more about what's going on. Start talking. Why are you here, and if you're in some kind of trouble, why didn't you call your brothers? Because I think you and I both know I'm the last person on earth you'd come to for help."

She didn't disagree with that, but another sound left her mouth. A hoarse sob. And that was when tears sprang to her eyes. "Please, let me see him."

He wasn't immune to those tears, and it gave him a tug of a different kind, one he didn't want. "Tell me what's going on," Cameron repeated.

Lauren frantically shook her head. "There isn't time."

Cameron huffed in frustration. "Then make time. Is someone after you? And what does that have to do with Gilly's son?"

She stared at him, her mouth trembling now, and those tears still watering her eyes. "Someone tried to kill me."

That put him on full alert, and he automatically caught on to her arm and pulled her behind him. Cameron positioned himself in between her and the area where she kept glancing.

"Keep talking," he insisted. He didn't see anyone out there, but the woods were fairly thick here. "When and where did this happen?"

Again, no fast answer. Which it should have been. After all, a murder attempt should have been fresh enough in her mind that Lauren could have rattled off the details.

"Last night," she finally said. "Two armed men broke into my house in Dallas and shot me."

The profanity flew out of his mouth before Cameron could stop it, and he whirled around just as she pulled back the collar of her dark blue button-up shirt. There was a bandage there. A bandage covering what had to be a sensitive wound judging by the way Lauren winced when she moved her shoulder.

"I'm okay," she added. "Well, physically anyway. The bullet only clipped me, and I was able to get away from them."

Good. But that didn't cause Cameron to feel any relief. "What about your son? Was he hurt?"

"No. There was a panic room in the house, and I had his nanny take him there right after the burglar alarm went off. I didn't manage to get in there in time before they got to me." She paused, choked back a sob. "I heard them say they had orders to kill me. And it wasn't a case of mistaken identity or anything. They said my name."

That did it. He took hold of her hand. "Come on. I'm taking you to Gabriel right now."

But Lauren pulled away from him. "No. Not yet

anyway. Not until I know it's safe. I also heard the men say they were cops."

Cameron stared at her. "Cops? Maybe. Criminals don't always tell the truth, but even if they had, your brother's not dirty."

Even though she didn't come out and say it, she'd once suspected Cameron of being just that—dirty. He hadn't been, but Lauren had deemed him guilty by association. Because he'd been friends with the family of the man who'd murdered her parents. If that friendship hadn't existed, then her mom and dad might still be alive.

Somehow, Cameron had never learned to live with that.

"Gabriel and Jameson aren't behind this," she said. "Whatever *this* is," Lauren added in a mumble. "But if those men were really cops and they know all about me, then they must figure I'd go to my lawmen brothers." Another pause, and she dodged his gaze. "This is the last place they'd expect me to come."

True. It wasn't exactly a secret about Lauren's hatred for him. But that wasn't hatred he was seeing in her eyes now. It was fear. Cameron was certain he was feeling some of that, as well. Fear for her. But there were still some very weird things going on.

"Where's your son now?" he asked.

That was concern number one. Once Lauren and the child were safe, then he could work out the rest with her. The *rest* would include bringing in her brothers on this. No way would Gabriel and Jameson want to be left out when someone was gunning for their kid sister, and it didn't matter if they were estranged from Lauren.

She fluttered her fingers in the direction of the trail. "He's in the car with the nanny. That's why I can't stay. I have to get back to him."

Yeah, she did, and Cameron would go with her. "Take me to him, and I can bring all three of you inside while we work this out."

She did more of that frantic head-shaking. "Not yet. Not until I know. Not until I'm sure I can trust you."

Cameron pulled back his shoulders. Trust had indeed been an issue between them in the past. Her trust for him anyway. But from what he could see in the depths of her eyes, this went beyond their past.

"If you didn't trust me, why come here?" he snapped. And he hated how much it stung that this bad blood was still between them.

"I didn't have a choice." Her voice cracked. "I need to see Isaac."

There it was again—something else she'd said that didn't make sense. Or maybe it did. Cameron hadn't been with Gilly when she'd died from a blood clot less than twenty-four hours after giving birth. He'd still been on the road trying to get to her in Dallas. Lauren had been there, though. Maybe had even spoken to her since Lauren and his sister had remained friends. Not only that, they'd lived in the same city.

"Did Gilly tell you something before she died?"

It was the same tone he used to interrogate a suspect. Not an especially friendly one, but he wanted answers, and Lauren was going to give them to him now.

Lauren's mouth opened a little to let him know the question had surprised her. Well, welcome to the club. He'd been surprised by a lot of what Lauren had said.

"No," she answered after several long moments. "This isn't about Gilly. This is about her son. Does he look like her or like his father?"

Now it was Cameron's turn to take a moment before he responded. "I never met his father, Trace Waters. Never wanted to meet him."

She made a sound of agreement, which meant Lauren knew that Trace had been abusive. Something that Gilly hadn't told Cameron until it was too late for him to go to Dallas and beat the living daylights out of the moron for laying a hand on his kid sister. By the time Cameron had heard, Trace had disappeared. Then, several weeks after Gilly had died, someone else had taken it beyond the beating stage and had killed Trace in a drug deal gone wrong.

"Trace's mother, Evelyn, came to the ranch once," Cameron explained. "She pulled a gun on me and demanded her son's baby." He felt his mouth tighten. "I don't like it when people pull guns on me so I had her arrested. The moment she made bail I slapped her with a restraining order."

"And that worked? Evelyn stayed away?"

He shook his head. "She tried to get on the grounds a couple of times, but the hands spotted her and stopped her. After the third time, she ended up in jail, where she's spent the last four months."

Cameron hoped the woman would do something behind bars that would keep her there. He wasn't concerned about losing custody to her. Gilly had made it clear to the hospital staff that she'd wanted Cameron to raise her son. But he didn't want Evelyn to be a free woman so she could try something else stupid.

"Does Isaac look like Gilly?" Lauren pressed. "Or anyone else in your family?"

Cameron nearly said no, but Lauren wasn't getting answers until he had some from her. "Let's get your baby and the nanny into the house, and we can talk."

"He doesn't look like Gilly," she said like gospel. "Or Trace."

Cameron lifted his shoulder. "Lots of kids don't look like their parents. Plus, he's a baby. Only thirteen months old." He huffed, scrubbing his hand over his forehead. "Look, I don't know where this is going, but I can have Gabriel come out—"

Only because he wasn't expecting it, Cameron didn't see Lauren pull that gun from the back of her jeans.

And she pointed it at him.

His heart slammed against his ribs. Damn. He should have been able to stop this before it'd even started, but Cameron fought the instinct to lunge at her and snatch that gun from her hand. He sure as hell wasn't pleased about this, though.

"What do you think you're doing?" he demanded once he got his teeth unclenched.

"I'm saving my son." Lauren used the barrel of the weapon to motion toward the house. "And you'll take me to him. I want to see Isaac now."

Chapter Two

Lauren saw exactly what she'd expected to see in Cameron's eyes.

Anger.

There was plenty of it, too, along with the shock of having her pull a gun on him. This certainly wasn't the way Lauren had wanted all of this to play out, but she hadn't exactly had a lot of options. The seconds were ticking away.

"Move," she ordered Cameron in the strongest voice she could manage. Which wasn't much. She didn't feel strong at all. Just terrified.

This couldn't be happening.

Over the past decade, she'd accepted that she could be in danger from the lunatic who kept sending those threatening letters, but she couldn't accept that two innocent babies could now be in harm's way.

"Put down the gun," Cameron warned her. And it was indeed a warning. Unlike her, he had managed the strong tone, and it had a dark edge to it. An edge that reminded her that she was holding a cop—an experienced one—at gunpoint.

"I can't." She tried to make that sound like an apology and failed at it, too. "I need to see Isaac."

Of course, Cameron would want to know why, and Lauren would tell him. First, though, she had to see the baby.

"Can't?" he repeated, that edge in his voice going up a notch. It went up in his smoke-gray eyes, too.

When she'd been a teenager, the girls had called them bedroom eyes because he was so hot. Still was. With that dark blond hair and natural tan, he'd always had rock-star looks. Those looks were still there in spades, but there wasn't a trace of his bedroom smile.

"Please," Lauren tried. "Just let me see him, and I might be able to clear all of this up."

"You'll clear it up now." Again, it was a warning. "And if you don't, you won't get anywhere near my nephew. However, you will get to see the inside of a jail cell."

She had no idea if that was a threat or not. He certainly had grounds to arrest her, and the fact that they'd once been lovers might not be enough leverage to stop this situation from snowballing.

Cameron still had hold of his gun, but he used his left hand to reach for his pocket. For his phone, she realized. He was going to call one or both of her brothers, and she didn't want them involved in this yet. Not until she could at least try to make things safe.

"No!" she said.

It was the only thing she managed to get out of her mouth, though, because Cameron didn't take out his phone. He lunged at her. Fast. Before Lauren could even react and get out of his way, he rammed into her and sent them both to the ground. While they were still falling, he knocked her gun from her hand.

"Start talking right now," Cameron growled, and he pinned her hands to the ground so she couldn't reach for her gun. He pinned her, too, with his body since he was on top of her.

Lauren's heart was racing. Along with that, she got a new hit of adrenaline. Something she definitely didn't need since her nerves were already firing in every inch of her.

She looked at Cameron, their gazes colliding, and for a moment she remembered what had once been between them. The intimacy.

The love.

Yes, once she'd loved him, and she thought maybe he'd felt the same way about her, but it was obvious those emotions were long gone. Well, maybe not the heat that had first drawn them together, but he definitely wasn't having any warm and fuzzy feelings about her now.

Lauren struggled, trying to force him off her, but when it was obvious this was a losing battle, she knew she had to say something.

And that something was going to shatter the life Cameron had built here.

"Did I hurt you?" he asked, the question surprising her.

Only then did she remember the wound on her shoulder. That part of her hadn't hit the ground, thank goodness, and since it was a constant throbbing pain, it had become a sort of white noise. Something she was trying to push aside so it wouldn't cause her to lose focus.

"No. I'm not hurt." But in hindsight, she probably should have lied. Maybe then, Cameron would have let her go.

"Talk to me," he snapped. Obviously, he was over his concern for her injury. Of course, she couldn't blame him when there were so many other things for them to discuss.

"We're in danger," she started. Lauren had to clear her throat and repeat it so it'd have some sound. "Those men who tried to kill me got away, and I believe they'll be looking for me. Maybe for you, too."

Because he was right in her face, it wasn't hard to see the doubt go through his eyes. Despite the doubts, though, he still had a look around them. A cop's look. Good. Lauren didn't want anyone sneaking up on them. Or worse—trying to sneak into the house.

"What do those men have to do with me?" he snarled.

"Maybe everything."

She tried to gather her breath. Couldn't. Cameron wasn't overly muscled, but he wasn't a lightweight, either, and with his chest pressing against her, she couldn't get enough air. He must have realized that, but he didn't move. Probably because he thought she would go for her gun again.

Which she would.

Since there was no easy way to say this, Lauren just blurted it out. "I believe someone swapped my baby with Gilly's."

She gave him a moment to let that sink in, but she couldn't give him the time he needed. She also continued to keep watch as best she could. Hard to do that, though, while on the ground.

He shook his head. "Why would anyone do that?"

"I'm not sure. Please, let's just check on Isaac, and then we can go over all of this."

Cameron didn't answer. Not with words anyway. But his cold, hard stare told her that wasn't going to happen.

"Someone started following me days ago. Two men in a dark car," she added. "I believe those were the same men who broke into my house."

"The men who tried to kill you." Cameron said it as if he didn't believe her. She couldn't blame him. She'd had hours to try to come to grips with it, and part of her still wasn't ready to accept it.

She nodded. "Before they found me, I heard them talking to someone on a communicator, and that's when they said they were cops."

"They could have lied," he reminded her again.

"True. But they still broke in for a reason. And that reason was my son, Patrick. They wanted to kill me and take him." She huffed in frustration because his skeptical look was only getting worse, and she wasn't explaining this well at all. "Just please move off me so we can both keep watch."

She saw him debate that for several moments. Lauren had lost track of how long she'd been out here with him, but Dara, the nanny, would be getting even more worried than she already was.

"If you try anything else stupid, I will put you right back on the ground," Cameron growled.

He finally shifted his body to the side, rolling off her. He also snatched up her gun as he stood. Lauren didn't like not being armed, but at least when she got up, she was able to better keep an eye on the trail behind them.

"Does your nephew look like your sister?" she came out and asked.

He stopped glancing around long enough to shoot her a glare. "That proves nothing. He could have inherited genes from generations ago."

Lauren hesitated a moment. "Does he look like me?"

His quick glare intensified, but what he didn't do was deny it. "First, you have to convince me that a swap even took place before I'll start speculating about who my nephew does or doesn't resemble."

Fair enough. Or at least it would have been fair if time was on their side. She instinctively knew it wasn't.

"I was telling the truth when I said I can't be

sure a swap took place, but the men said once they had Patrick, they could do a DNA test and go from there. Go from there," she emphasized. "I believe that means they'll come here next."

Cameron cursed, and it wasn't tame. "That's a big leap to assume the men were talking about Isaac."

"A leap except that I'd already started to get suspicious. Patrick doesn't look like me or my late husband." She swallowed hard. "He looks like you."

She could tell from his slight flinch that Cameron reacted to that. Maybe because he saw something of her face in Isaac's?

"Gilly could have arranged the swap," Lauren went on. "She was afraid of Trace, and if she knew she was dying, this might have been her way of preventing Trace from getting his hands on their child."

Though it sickened her to think that Gilly, a woman she considered her friend, would have intentionally done something like this since it could have put Lauren's own precious son in danger.

"Gilly wouldn't do that," Cameron insisted. "If she was worried about her baby's safety, she would have gotten word to me."

"Maybe. But Gilly was dying. Scared. And they'd had trouble getting in touch with you."

He flinched again, and she knew why. Cameron had gotten caught up in a lockdown at the prison, where he'd gone to interview a potential witness. He'd been trapped there for hours with no way to leave and get to his sister even though she'd gone into labor.

"But Gilly might not have done this," Lauren added a moment later.

Mercy, she wished she'd rehearsed this or something because it was hard for her to put her line of thinking into words. Equally hard for her to imagine it had happened. "My late husband was Alden Lange, and his business partner or his sister could be the one responsible. They both hate me. Or at least they hate that I have control over Alden's estate."

The flat look Cameron gave her told her he wasn't buying that. And she hoped she was wrong. Because both Alden's sister, Julia, and his partner, Duane Tulley, could be very dangerous. They might have seen this as some sick mind game to watch her suffer. Of course, her suffering could also be profitable for them if it led to one or both of them getting their hands on Alden's money.

"How would Trace or any of these other people have gotten into the hospital nursery to switch babies?" he asked.

Lauren didn't have the answer to that, either. "It must have been an inside job since the babies wear bracelets with security chips that would trigger an alarm if they were carried out of the hospital. I'd just started checking out the medical staff when I was attacked."

He made a sound, a rumble deep in his throat. "And why did you do that? What made you suspicious?"

"I kept thinking it was strange that I would look at my son and see you." She waved that off before he could say anything about it. She didn't want to talk about why the image of Cameron's face was still so clear in her head after all these years and after all the bad stuff that'd gone on between them.

"I had a DNA test done," she went on. "So I could compare Patrick's DNA to mine. I'm supposed to get the results back any day now, but I made the mistake of asking the housekeeper if there was anything still around with Alden's DNA on it." She'd cursed herself for doing that. "I wanted to have the complete DNA results, but I think the housekeeper told Alden's sister what I'd asked for."

At least Cameron hadn't simply dismissed her. He tipped his head to the trail. "We'll get your son and sort this out." Lauren was about to blow out a breath of relief, but then Cameron added, "For the record, I don't believe there was a swap. Isaac is my nephew. But if Duane and Julia are bad news like you think they are, then they could have been the ones behind your attack."

He took her by the arm again to get her moving, but Lauren dug in her heels. "I can't risk bringing my brothers into this yet. Those thugs who attacked me could have connections to Duane and Julia, and they could find out I'm here."

This huff was even louder than his last one. "Look, Gabriel is the sheriff, and my boss. As well as your brother. No way would he risk putting you in danger.

I'll just go inside, call him on his personal line and have him come out here."

"No." She couldn't say that fast enough. "I heard those men say if my family got in the way, they would have to kill them."

She hated when his skeptical look returned. Because she had the same skepticism. "I know those thugs could have wanted me to hear what they were saying, that they could have been feeding me information. But why would they have done that, then shoot me and try to take Patrick?"

"That's what we'll find out—as soon as I call Gabriel." He tightened his grip on her arm and managed to drag her a few steps.

"They could be watching the front of your house from the road. They could be watching Gabriel's and Jameson's places, too. That's why I used the trail. Only the locals know it's there, and it's not easy to spot unless you're looking for it."

Cameron couldn't argue with that, not the last part anyway, even though it looked as if he wanted to dispute something. *Anything.* "We'll go in through the back of my house. Even hired guns won't be suspicious if they see the sheriff dropping by to visit with one of his deputies."

Lauren wasn't so sure of that at all. Anything out of the ordinary might trigger those men to shoot again. And this time, Isaac and anyone else who happened to be around could get hurt. If the gunmen were truly out there, they could be looking for any sign she was there, and Gabriel's visit might give her away.

"I shouldn't have come here," Lauren said under her breath. She lifted her head, making direct eye contact with Cameron. "But I just had to know if Isaac's really my son. Don't get me wrong. I love Patrick with all my heart, but I had to find out the truth."

Cameron hesitated, volleying glances at the house, the woods and her. Just when she thought he was about to give in and let her go inside, she heard something. Footsteps. Cameron heard them, too, because he pushed her behind him and aimed his gun in the direction of the sound.

Someone was running toward them.

Oh, God. Had something happened to Patrick?

Nothing could have kept Lauren behind Cameron. She snatched her gun from his left hand and would have taken off toward her car, but she finally saw something.

Something that stopped her cold.

Dara. The nanny had Patrick clutched to her chest, and she was running—fast. Probably as fast as she could go.

"They found us," Dara shouted. "Run!"

Chapter Three

Cameron hadn't been sure of what he was going to do, but there was no time left to debate it now. All of his lawman's instincts told him that the stark fear in the woman's voice was real.

So was that baby she had gripped in her arms.

A little blond-haired boy who was about the same size as Isaac.

Cameron forced himself not to think that everything Lauren had told him was real. If this was truly his nephew, anything he felt about that would have to wait. Right now he had to get them to safety.

"Get inside the house," Cameron told Lauren.

She didn't listen, of course. Neither would he if that'd been his child out there. Lauren started to run toward the nanny, but Cameron hurried in front of her. The moment he got to the woman and child, he hooked his arm around them, maneuvering them in front of him, and he got them running again.

"Keep watch around us," Cameron told Lauren.

Maybe that would stop the panic he saw rising

in her eyes. It was also something that needed to be done. Because if those two armed thugs were on their tail, then they had to get inside—fast—but they also needed to make sure they weren't about to be gunned down. If necessary, they would have to take cover before they even reached the house.

The little boy wasn't out and out crying, but he was whimpering. Probably because he'd picked up on their fear and because the running was jostling him. Cameron tried to ignore the sounds he was making, and he got them on the porch. He had to fumble in his pocket to get his keys to unlock the door, but the moment he did that, he pushed them inside.

"Get on the floor," he ordered.

Cameron relocked the door, set the security alarm and went to the window to keep watch. He also fired off a text to Gabriel, asking him to come over. Lauren's brother didn't live far and could be there in minutes if he hadn't already left for work. If so, then Gabriel would have to drive back.

A lot could happen in those extra minutes it would take Gabriel to do that.

Cameron still had a much too clear image of the bandage on Lauren's shoulder where she'd been shot. Those goons could be returning now to finish her off.

Lauren scrambled to the nanny, taking Patrick into her arms and pulling him close. There were tears in her eyes again, and she was trembling. The nanny wasn't faring much better. Hell, neither was he. Cameron wasn't trembling the way they were, but he was worried because they had two babies in the house, and he might not be able to protect them if those gunmen started shooting.

"I saw an SUV coming up the trail," the nanny said. Her breath was gusting so hard that it was difficult to understand her. "I couldn't drive off since there were trees blocking the way so I got out and started running with Patrick."

Yeah, there were downed trees back there. Probably shrubs, too, since it wasn't a trail that was often used.

"It could turn out to be nothing," the nanny added in a hoarse whisper. "They might not be the men who were after us."

Judging from her tone, she didn't think that was true. Neither did Cameron. It was too much of a coincidence for someone to show up on that trail so soon after Lauren had been shot.

"Did you get a glimpse of anyone in the SUV?" he asked the woman.

"Barely. I could just make out the outline of the driver behind the tinted glass. I think there was another man in the passenger seat."

Maybe the same two who had attacked Lauren in Dallas. If so, they'd come a long way. And they had probably had some inside help since Lauren had been right about the trail. Not many people outside the area knew it existed. Of course, a police officer might know because they could have tapped into the area maps that were in the database at San Antonio PD.

Hell, he hoped they weren't dealing with dirty cops.

"Is everything okay?" someone called out from the other side of the house. Merilee.

That tightened the knot in his stomach. He could tell Merilee was terrified, as well. She'd been Isaac's nanny right from the start, and since there'd already been two attacks on the ranch, she knew something was wrong.

"Just stay put in the nursery," Cameron settled for saying. He didn't want to unnecessarily alarm the woman even though she was probably well past the alarm stage already.

Cameron also had a second reason for keeping Merilee and Isaac where they were. This way, Lauren wouldn't see Isaac. Of course, she would see him soon enough, but right now he needed her to focus. If Lauren saw him and truly believed he was her son, then she might fall apart.

"Hand Patrick to Dara," Cameron told Lauren. "I need you to keep watch at the window on the side of the house."

He hated to ask her to do that, but right now she was their best bet. Besides, he knew Lauren could shoot since he'd been the one to teach her.

She gave a shaky nod, passed the baby back to the nanny and with a tight grip on her gun, she went to the window near the breakfast table. He didn't have to remind her to stay back. She did. Lauren positioned herself against the side of the glass so she could still peer out.

"Nothing," she relayed to him.

It was the same from his view. That didn't mean the men weren't out there, though. Lauren had been out there for a while before he'd spotted her. Plus, it was possible the men were regrouping, maybe calling for their own backup so they could storm the place and take the baby.

But why?

That was something he intended to find out once they were out of any immediate danger.

Behind him, Patrick started fussing, and he made the mistake of glancing back at the boy. Cameron hadn't been able to see his face earlier when the nanny was running toward them. He saw it now, though.

Oh, man.

It felt like someone had knocked the breath right out of him. The kid had blond hair, and those were definitely the Doran gray eyes. In fact, the resemblance was close enough that Patrick could have been mistaken for Cameron's own son. He wasn't.

But the boy was his nephew.

Cameron silently cursed. This was not what he wanted in his head right now, but it was a fight to keep the thoughts at bay. What the hell was he going to do?

He forced his attention back to the window just

as the sound shot through the room. Clearly, everyone was on edge because both Lauren and the nanny gasped. But it wasn't a shot being fired. It was just his phone ringing, and Cameron saw Gabriel's name on the screen. Good. Maybe that meant the sheriff was there.

Cameron put the call on speaker, laying his phone on the counter so his hands would be free in case there was an attack.

"What the hell is going on?" Gabriel demanded the moment he came onto the line.

Since he wasn't going to have time to get into everything, Cameron went with the short version. "Lauren's here, and some men are after her. They tried to kill her."

Gabriel cursed, but he quickly reined it in, no doubt because he realized his kid sister was listening. "Any reason she came to you and not me?"

Gabriel didn't rein in his emotions on that question. Cameron heard the anger come through loud and clear. The emotion was in Lauren's expression, too. Her forehead was bunched up, and she had her still-trembling bottom lip clamped between her teeth. With everything else she was facing, she probably didn't want a showdown with her brother, as well, but it was going to be on the agenda whether she wanted it or not.

"I'll explain it all later," Cameron told him, but he had to raise his voice to speak over Patrick. The baby was fussing even louder now. "The men who are after Lauren will be in an SUV," he added to Gabriel. "It's possible they're on the trail behind my house."

"They're not. I just spotted a black SUV coming up from the back of my folks' old place."

Cameron bit back a groan. The trails coiled all around the ranch, and the men had obviously found a way out of the woods. That meant they could be trying to escape so they could regroup and come at Lauren again. As much as Cameron hated the notion of that, at least it would give him a chance to get the babies, nannies and her to a safe place.

"The SUV isn't moving," Gabriel went on, "and I can't tell if anyone is still inside it. They could have already gotten out and slipped onto the ranch grounds."

Not exactly a comforting thought, but Gabriel was right. Cameron didn't know how long it'd taken the nanny to get to Lauren and him, but the thugs could have driven off the moment she started running. If so, that would have given them plenty of time to get to the old Beckett house, and then the chance to escape.

Or sneak up on Cameron's house.

"I've stopped on the road and am waiting for Jameson," Gabriel continued a moment later. "Once he's here, we can go closer. Why do they want Lauren?" he tacked onto that.

"She's not sure yet." But it gnawed away at him to think it could be because of his sister's scummy dead boyfriend. "Just give me a heads-up if you see these clowns."

"Will do. Is that Isaac crying?"

"No. It's…Lauren's son." Cameron hadn't meant to hesitate, but it'd just seemed to stick in his throat.

Gabriel's silence let Cameron know it hadn't been easy for him to hear. That was probably because Lauren hadn't bothered to introduce her son to the rest of her family. Even though things had been strained between Lauren and him since their parents' murders, it still had to cut Gabriel to the core. For him, it was all about family, and he'd worked damn hard to bring his siblings back to their birthplace.

Cameron ended the call, and he went to the back door to look out the small windows there. The angle was better for giving him a view of the opposite side of the yard that Lauren was watching. The SUV was the other direction, but it didn't mean the thugs couldn't have brought some help along.

"I think I see something," Lauren said.

That sent Cameron running to her, and he followed her pointing finger in the direction of the far side of his barn. Since the barn was closer to the old Beckett house than Cameron's, it would be a likely place for someone to hide.

But he didn't see anything.

"I'm obviously on edge," Lauren admitted. "It could have been my imagination."

She looked up at him at the exact moment he looked down at her, and it seemed as if there was something else she wanted to say to him. An apology, maybe, but the silence said it all. Because she'd been giving him the silent treatment for the past decade. No reason for this to be any different.

He kept watch, but even though he didn't see anything, it didn't mean someone wasn't out there. Which made him rethink their position. There were way too many windows in this part of the house. Plus, it was hard to hear anything with Patrick crying.

"Stay low," Cameron instructed the nanny, "but take the baby to the nursery. It's the first room off the hall." He tipped his head in that direction. "Go with them," he added to Lauren.

But she shook her head. "You need me to help you keep watch. I don't want those men getting in the house."

Neither did he, but Cameron had figured she'd want to be with her baby. And she probably did. However, like him, Lauren almost certainly knew things could turn on a dime.

"Merilee?" he called out. "A woman and little boy are joining you in the nursery. Once they're in there, lock the door, and all of you get down on the floor."

"What's happening?" Merilee asked. "Are you okay?"

"I'm fine. Lauren is here," he said after a pause.

Merilee would remember Lauren since she'd been the Beckett housekeeper all the way up until the time of the murders. Lauren's mom was a former cop who also worked the ranch, and Merilee had been a pseudo-nanny to Lauren and her siblings.

He nearly asked about Isaac, to make sure his nephew was all right, but right now Cameron only wanted to focus on what was going on outside. Besides, if something had been wrong in the nursery, Merilee would have let him know.

"Thank you," Lauren whispered.

Cameron was about to tell her not to thank him yet, but the movement stopped him cold. This time he saw what Lauren had almost certainly spotted by the barn.

A man.

He only got a glimpse of him, but the guy was wearing camo. Definitely not a ranch hand.

"He's got a gun," Lauren relayed to Cameron.

Yeah, he'd seen it, too. Again, just a glimpse, but it appeared to be a rifle. Not good because it gave the intruder a longer range that he could use to shoot into the house.

Without taking his attention off the man, Cameron pressed redial on his phone, and Gabriel answered on the first ring.

"Jameson's here," Gabriel explained. "We're going to the SUV now."

"Don't. One of the shooters is here at my place by the side of my barn. I figure he's not alone."

Gabriel made a sound of agreement followed by some profanity. "Okay, we're on the way to your place. I'll also get some of the hands over there."

"Tell them to be careful. The guy is armed, and he's in position to pick off anyone who comes up the road to my house."

And that was probably the reason he was there. Which made that bad feeling inside him go up a significant notch. If these goons knew the trail, maybe they'd watched the place. Perhaps his house. It wouldn't have been hard to do. On any given day there were at least two dozen hands working the ranch along with deliveries and the normal traffic that came with a place this size.

There could be gunmen waiting to ambush Gabriel, Jameson and anyone else who came this way.

Because if their ultimate goal was to get the baby, then it wouldn't matter how many people they killed.

He hated to put something else on Lauren's shoulders, but he needed an extra pair of eyes at the front of the house. That meant he'd have to stay to keep watch of the thug by the barn. Cameron was about to give her instructions as to what to do, but the blur of motion stopped him.

There was a second gunman at the back of the barn.

Unlike his partner, this one didn't immediately duck back behind cover. He lifted his rifle and fired. The shot crashed through the window right where Cameron was standing.

Chapter Four

Lauren shouted for Cameron to get down, but it was already too late. The gunman had fired the shot, the bullet blasting through the window.

In the blink of an eye, she saw a piece of glass slice across Cameron's arm. He was wearing a shirt, and she could immediately see the blood start to spread across the sleeve.

She ran to him, but Lauren wasn't quite able to reach his arm. That was because Cameron took hold of her and dragged her to the floor. But he didn't stay there. He got right back up and took aim out the now gaping hole in the window.

"You're hurt," she said, her breath gusting so hard that Lauren had trouble speaking.

"I'm okay," he grumbled.

But she had no idea if that was true. She couldn't tell if the glass was still in his arm or not because of all the blood.

From the other side of the house, Lauren heard a sound she didn't want to hear. Patrick was crying.

Probably because the noise from the gunshot had frightened him. She considered going to him, but she didn't want to leave Cameron alone. She got confirmation that would be a bad idea when two more shots came through the window. These slammed into the side of the fridge.

"Merilee!" Cameron called out to the nanny. "All of you need to get down on the floor and stay there." He glanced at her then, letting Lauren know that applied to her, too.

However, she shook her head. "If I go to the side window, I might have a clear shot and be able to stop the gunman."

"Yeah, and he might have a shot to stop you. Stay down," he repeated, this time through clenched teeth. She couldn't tell if the tight expression was for her or because he was grimacing in pain.

Lauren huffed. She'd forgotten just how stubborn Cameron could be, but this brought it all back. Worse, he didn't stay out of the line of fire. He leaned away from the wall, took aim out the window and pulled the trigger.

The blast echoed through the room. Through the entire house. And Lauren heard both babies cry. She prayed the nannies could keep the boys as calm as possible, but better yet, she just wanted the women to protect them so that none of the bullets could make it to them.

Her son was in danger.

Both her sons.

Because Isaac might be hers by blood, but Patrick was also hers in every way that mattered. Now the babies were at huge risk, and she didn't even know why. That was what cut away at her right now. That, and the bullets that continued to tear into the house.

She thought of what Cameron had said earlier. About Trace's mother, Evelyn, pulling a gun on him. And Lauren wondered if she was behind this. But she couldn't be. For one thing, the woman was in jail, and for another, she wanted custody of her grandson and almost certainly wouldn't put him at risk like this.

But Julia or Duane were capable of that.

They wouldn't have nearly the level of concern for Patrick or any other child that Evelyn likely would. In fact, it would make things easier for Julia or Duane if Lauren and her son were out of the way.

That certainly didn't help her raw nerves.

However, there was a third player in all of this. The idiot who was sending those threatening messages to her and her family. If so, they didn't have a clue who they were dealing with, and that person might not care if everyone inside the house died in a gunfight.

Cameron fired another shot, and he followed it with some profanity. "He's ducked back behind the barn."

Probably because Cameron's shots were getting too close to him. Lauren doubted, though, that the man was retreating. No. He was probably regrouping or else contacting his comrade so he could come at them from a different angle.

Cameron ran to the side of the room where Lauren had been earlier, but the moment he made it to that window, the gunman sent more bullets their way. That created yet another spray of glass over the room and caused Cameron to scramble back. Thankfully, he didn't get cut this time, and the bleeding on his arm seemed to be slowing down. Still, he needed medical attention. That wasn't going to happen, though, until those gunmen were stopped. No way could an ambulance risk coming to the house, since they would drive right into gunfire.

Cameron's phone rang, the sound somehow making it through the deafening blasts. He glanced at the screen and tossed it to her. "It's Gabriel. Let him know what's going on and find out his location."

Lauren cursed her trembling hands because it took her precious seconds to hit the answer button, and she put it on speaker so that Cameron could hear.

"Is everyone okay?" Gabriel asked right off.

"No. Cameron's hurt. His arm is bleeding— "

"I'm fine," Cameron snarled. "I've got a shooter by the barn and another out by the road."

That sped up her heartbeat even more because her brothers would be coming up that road to get to them. She prayed they didn't get hurt, or worse.

"Yeah, I've already spotted the one on the road," Gabriel answered. "That's why Jameson and I stopped.

The guy's in the ditch. If he lifts his head enough, Jameson can take him out."

Good. Except that would mean Jameson would have to take a huge risk to do that. Lauren had no idea if that guy was firing at her brothers or not. It was hard to tell with all the bullets flying.

"What about you?" Gabriel continued. "Can you shoot the one by the barn?"

"Haven't managed it so far, but I can't keep letting him fire bullets into the house."

No, they couldn't. Each one was a huge risk to the babies. And that meant she needed to push aside her fears and do something. She was the daughter and sister of a sheriff and had had firearms training. While she certainly didn't have experience in finishing off hired guns, she had plenty of motivation to put an end to this.

"Are there only two of them?" Gabriel asked a moment later.

Good question, and she could tell from Cameron's frustrated sigh that he didn't know the answer. "Two men attacked your sister last night and shot her in the arm so I'm guessing it's the same pair."

Gabriel cursed again, and Lauren recognized that tone after all these years. He was furious, and that fury wasn't limited to only these men, either. As her brother and the sheriff, he would have expected her to come to him with this. Later, she'd need to explain why she hadn't done that. But that would have to wait.

"I can try to distract the shooter by firing out the kitchen window," Lauren offered. "That way Cameron can try to get him from the front of the house."

That offer didn't please Cameron. It earned her a scowl, but she gave him one right back. "As you said, we can't let him keep firing shots."

She could see the debate Cameron was having with himself about that, but before he could say anything, his phone beeped, indicating he had another call coming in.

"It's from an unknown number," she relayed to him.

"Answer your phone, Deputy," the gunman shouted from outside. The shots also stopped. "We gotta talk."

"The thug by the barn is calling me," Cameron told Gabriel. "While I see what he wants, try to do something about the guy in the ditch. I don't want him getting any closer to the house."

"We'll do what we can," Gabriel assured him.

Lauren pressed the button to take the second call, and she crawled even closer to Cameron so he wouldn't miss a word of what this snake had to say.

"Are you ready to put an end to this?" the gunman asked without any hesitation. "Because I've got a solution that'll make sure your nephew and that other little boy don't get hurt."

"Who are you?" Cameron snapped.

"You don't need to know my name to listen to what I got to say."

"No, but I do need to know who hired you so I

can put his or her butt in jail for multiple accounts of attempted murder."

The guy chuckled. "Let's just say that's not gonna happen and move on. You want me to stop shooting up your house, then here's what you have to do. Put Lauren on the phone so the two of us can talk this out."

A chill slid through her. Of course the goon knew she was there, but it was still stomach-twisting to hear him say her name. She opened her mouth to tell him she was listening, but Cameron shook his head and shot her a warning glance.

"Anything you think you need to say to Lauren, you can say to me," Cameron told the gunman.

"I don't think so. Something tells me you're not gonna be nearly as easy to reason with as she'll be." Considering his casual tone, he could have been discussing the weather, but Lauren knew there was nothing casual about any of this.

"You want money, is that it?" she asked.

That didn't please Cameron. No surprise there. He mumbled some profanity and hurried to the other side of the window—probably hoping he could get off a shot while the gunman was talking.

"Money?" the gunman repeated as if it was a joke. "No, sugar. Money ain't gonna fix this."

She hated his flippant attitude and wished she could be the one to silence him. But Lauren wanted that silence only after they'd learned who had hired this monster. Then him, his partner and his boss could be arrested.

"What, then?" she demanded, and Lauren hoped she sounded less shaky than she felt.

"I want you, sugar."

For just a handful of words, they packed a punch along with making her skin crawl. She wasn't sure if he'd meant for it to sound sexual or not.

"All you have to do is walk out the back door," the gunman continued. "Of course, I'm gonna want your hands in the air so I can make sure you don't have a gun. And I'll also want you to tell the deputy that he's out of the picture right now."

"You're not going out there," Cameron told her before the gunman had even finished.

"Figured you'd feel that way, but just think about those little kids. Do I hear them crying? Bet they're real scared, but they're gonna get a lot more scared when I start shooting again. Because once I start, I won't stop until I've ripped your place to shreds. You got thirty seconds, or the bullets start up again."

Lauren sucked in her breath so hard that she nearly choked, and she managed to get to her feet.

"No." Cameron hurried toward her, catching on to her and pulling her down against the fridge. He also took his phone from her and hit the end call button. "He'll gun you down the moment you step outside."

She shook her head, not disputing that since she figured that was exactly what would happen. Someone wanted her dead.

"But if I don't go out there, he'll shoot into the house," she reminded Cameron, though she was certain he hadn't forgotten that.

"He'll do it anyway." He took hold of her chin, lifting it and forcing eye contact. Brief eye contact, just enough for her to see the determination in his eyes before he went back to the window to keep watch. "Think it through. He'll have to kill me, too, so he can escape. In fact, this plan could be about me. A way to draw me out while using you. Because that snake knows I won't let you go to your death."

That last part was definitely true. Cameron wasn't a coward, and he was married to that badge he had clipped to his holster. He would put his own life ahead of hers or anyone else's that he needed to protect.

She tried to figure out if that was indeed what the gunman had in mind, but the thoughts were flying through her head, making it hard to think. The only thing that was coming through loud and clear was that she had to do something, anything, to save the babies.

Cameron glanced around, too, as if trying to sort out what to do, and he finally tipped his head to the front of the house. "Take your gun and go to the window in there. Stay to the side, but if you get a shot, take it."

She didn't thank him. In fact, Lauren didn't say anything for fear he would change his mind. As she was leaving, she heard him make a quick call to

Gabriel to tell him to do something to eliminate the guy in the ditch.

Lauren's pulse was thudding so hard now that it was hard to hear, and her feet felt heavy, as if she was trudging through mud. Still, she moved as fast as she could and tried to ignore the sounds of the babies crying. She had to focus, had to do her part to make this right. Then she could deal with the fallout of the baby swap and everything else that her homecoming would cause.

There were three windows in the living room. A huge one that faced the front and two side ones that had a view of the barn. She went to the one that she hoped would give her the best vantage point.

It did.

She immediately caught a glimpse of the gunman, and he was lifting his rifle, pointing it right at the house. That put her heart in her throat. She hadn't needed anything to add to the urgency of their situation, but that did it anyway.

Lauren didn't waste even a second. She broke the glass with the barrel of her gun and took aim. The gunman shifted his position, trying to turn his weapon at her. But it was too late.

She fired.

And she was right on target. The bullet slammed into the guy's chest. He stayed there, frozen and crouched, his rifle ready, but neither he nor his gun moved. So, Lauren shot him again.

He finally dropped like a stone.

Despite the fact that she'd probably just killed a man, she only felt relief and not the emotion of having just taken a life. That was because if he'd been given the chance, he would have killed them all.

She heard the footsteps, hurrying toward her. Cameron. From his angle in the kitchen, he probably hadn't been able to see the fall, but he certainly saw it now. There was no relief on his face, though, because they heard something else.

Another shot.

This one hadn't come from the barn. It had come from the front of the house, and it wasn't a single shot, either. Three more quickly followed.

There was no trace of relief now for Lauren. Because she knew her brothers were in the general direction of that fresh round of bullets. Maybe the gunman's partner had figured out what had gone on by the barn and was now trying to take out anyone that he could.

Lauren turned to run to the front window, but Cameron moved in front of her. "Watch the guy you shot and make sure he doesn't get up."

She was about to tell him that she doubted that could happen, but there was more gunfire. Then Cameron cursed when he looked out the front window.

"Change of plans," he said. "Get down now."

There was more than enough urgency in his voice for Lauren to drop to the floor, but she'd barely had time to do that when Cameron threw open the front door. The security system started to beep, indicating the alarm was about to go off. He ignored that, though, aimed his gun and fired. He got off four rounds before he stopped pulling the trigger.

Lauren waited, praying and afraid to ask what had happened. Several moments later she heard something she actually wanted to hear.

Gabriel's voice.

"Is everyone okay?" her brother called out.

Since the babies were still fussing, Lauren knew they were alive, but she got up to hurry to the nursery to make sure. But she stopped when she saw the chaos in front of Cameron's house.

Two men dressed in camo were sprawled out by the ditch. The one nearest the house was clearly dead, but the other one was still moving around. Both Jameson and Gabriel had their weapons drawn and were closing in on him.

Her stomach sank. Lauren hadn't even known about the third gunman. He could have attacked them from the front while the thug by the barn was keeping them occupied. Thank God Cameron and her brothers had spotted him and stopped him from doing any more harm.

"I had to shoot him," Cameron said. He pressed in the numbers on the security key pad to stop the beeping. "I didn't have a choice."

It took her a moment to realize why that sounded like an apology. It was because two of their attackers were dead, and the third one was injured. Maybe even dying. Dead men wouldn't be able to tell them the person or the reason behind what had just happened.

"Stay inside," Cameron added. "But keep watch to make sure there aren't others."

Lauren hadn't exactly relaxed, but that put her back on high alert again. So did the fact that Cameron hurried outside. Where he could be gunned down like her brothers if there were other thugs hiding.

Even though Cameron had told her to stay inside, Lauren got her gun ready and stepped into the doorway so she'd have a better view of the yard and road. Her brothers were already by the injured man by the time Cameron reached them. She could see them talking, but she couldn't hear what they were saying.

But she had no trouble seeing the alarm on Cameron's face.

Whatever the man had said to him had caused Cameron's shoulders to snap back. Her brothers had similar reactions, and Gabriel took out his phone as he made his way to the house. Cameron and Jameson were right behind him. That was when Lauren realized the injured man was no longer moving.

Gabriel made eye contact with her, and while he continued his phone conversation, he caught on to her arm and maneuvered her back inside the house.

"What about the man?" she asked.

"He's dead," Cameron told her the moment he reached the porch.

The sickening feeling of dread went through her. "Did he say anything?" But Lauren fully expected that answer to be no.

It wasn't.

Cameron nodded. "He gave us the name of the person who hired him." His mouth tightened when he made eye contact with Lauren. "The gunman said it was *you*."

Chapter Five

"I didn't hire those men," Lauren repeated.

It wasn't necessary for her to keep saying that. Cameron hadn't believed it from the moment the thug had tossed out that stupid accusation. Those men had been firing real bullets into the house as well as at Lauren and him, and there was no way she would have put her son in danger that way.

Either son.

Because Cameron was also certain she was already thinking of both boys as hers. They weren't. But that was something they would have to sort out later.

For now, they needed to get to the bottom of why the attack had happened. Gabriel and Jameson were already on that. Lauren's brothers were outside with the medical examiner and the CSIs. The ambulance, too. There'd been no need for medical assistance for the gunmen—they were all dead. But the medics were apparently there for Lauren and him.

Whether they wanted them there or not.

Cameron certainly didn't. He wanted to be outside with the other lawmen, trying to get answers, but instead he was on the sofa in his living room while a medic stitched up his arm. Another medic was checking out Lauren's gunshot wound, as well.

"This isn't necessary," Lauren insisted. It was yet something else she'd been repeating.

Cameron didn't bother to voice his complaint since Gabriel had told him he wouldn't be returning to work until the medic gave him the okay. So far, the guy wasn't okaying anything. He was causing Cameron plenty of pain with each stitch. Of course, that was a small price to pay considering they were all alive and, for the most part, well.

"Is it okay if we come out now?" Merilee called out.

It had been well over a half hour since the attack had ended. If the thugs had brought any other hired guns with them, those guys would probably be long gone. But it still seemed too big of a risk to take.

"Let's call this finished," Cameron told the medic, and even though the guy gave him a hard look, he put in the last stitch and slapped on a bandage.

"Stay put. I'll come to the nursery," Cameron added to Merilee.

That got Lauren moving, too, and despite the fact that the medic was still dabbing something on her arm, she jerked away from him, following Cameron when he started out of the living room and up the hall. Both medics grumbled something that Cameron didn't bother to hear. He needed to see Isaac to make sure for himself that both boys were all right.

Lauren was right on his heels when Cameron knocked on the door. Merilee must have been right there waiting because she opened up right away. She didn't have Isaac in her arms, but Cameron spotted him. He was on the floor, playing with Patrick. Dara was next to both of them.

Cameron felt the punch of relief. Yes, he'd known the boys hadn't been harmed. He'd gotten that reassurance minutes after the attack when he'd been able to talk to Merilee. So had Lauren. But she also must have needed more because she hurried to the boys, kissing them both.

Kisses that got Merilee's attention.

The nanny looked at him, her eyebrow raised. "I'll explain later," Cameron whispered to her. "Thanks for keeping them safe."

"Is it actually safe?" Merilee questioned before Cameron could step away.

"No," he admitted after a pause. "We don't know who hired those men."

And he needed to figure out what to do about that. His house was in too vulnerable of a spot on the ranch since it was backed up against the woods and those trails. Added to that, there were now broken windows, so he would need to move Lauren, the boys and the nannies. First, though, he needed to see Isaac.

The boys were no longer fussing. In fact, they

were looking a little confused—Isaac, especially—
at the long hug that Lauren was giving them. When
Cameron sank down on the edge of one of the chairs,
Isaac scooted out of her grip and immediately went
to him.

"Nunk," Isaac babbled. It was his attempt at uncle,
and it always made Cameron smile. Even more. And
while he hugged Isaac often, this hug was especially
needed.

Of course, Isaac didn't let the hug go on for long.
He was a kid always on the go, and the moment
Cameron stood him on the floor, Isaac toddled his
way back to Patrick. He dropped down next to him,
where there was a huge pile of toy cars and horses.

Seeing them side by side put a knot in Cameron's
stomach. If he'd had any doubts about the baby swap,
he didn't have them now. He could see his sister, and
himself, in Patrick's face, while Isaac was a Beckett. Cameron hadn't seen it before because he hadn't
been looking for it.

Hell.

What was he going to do now?

Lauren looked up at him at the exact moment
that Cameron looked at her. She didn't say anything,
but she seemed to be waiting for something. Maybe
for him to offer some perfect solution to fix all of
this. But at the moment he was drawing a blank because the one thing he wasn't going to do was give
up the little boy he'd been raising for over a year.

He couldn't have loved his own son more than he loved Isaac.

Cameron automatically reached for his gun again when he heard someone coming up the hall. He stood, stepping in front of the others, but it wasn't a threat this time. It was Gabriel and Jameson.

Lauren stood, slowly, and she rubbed her hands along the sides of her jeans. Her brothers didn't exactly run to her, either, and Cameron figured they needed some time to hash this out. After all, Lauren had basically abandoned them, but again, that was something that would have to wait.

"Cameron told us about the possible baby switch," Gabriel said, his voice not exactly warm and fuzzy.

She looked at Cameron, probably wondering when he'd had a chance to do that. It'd been in the yard when he'd managed to have a very short conversation with Gabriel while they were waiting for the medics to arrive. And Cameron had indeed added that word—*possible*. But Gabriel and Jameson were no doubt seeing what Cameron had—Patrick's resemblance to them.

Jameson huffed, went to Lauren and pulled her into his arms. "You shouldn't have stayed away," he whispered to her, but since the room was suddenly quiet, Cameron had no trouble hearing.

"I couldn't," she answered. When Lauren pulled back, she was blinking back tears. "Not after what happened to Mom and Dad. I just couldn't stay."

Gabriel didn't argue with that. Not with his voice

anyway. But that wasn't exactly a forgiving look in his eyes.

Of course, Cameron hadn't expected there to be. Like Gabriel and Jameson, he'd stayed in Blue River. He'd dealt with the aftermath, had helped put a killer behind bars and then had tried to pick up the pieces and use them to build a new life. Lauren hadn't done that, and it'd cut Gabriel to the core that he hadn't been able to keep the family together.

"Uh, should Dara and I take the boys to one of the other rooms?" Merilee asked after glancing at Gabriel's expression.

"No," Lauren answered without hesitation. Cameron agreed. He didn't want the babies out of his sight for now. If Lauren's brothers were going to have words with her, they'd have to keep it G-rated.

Lauren kissed Jameson on the cheek, and she went to Gabriel. Her steps were tentative and so was the kiss on the cheek she gave him.

"I don't expect you to understand what I did," she said, her voice a little shaky now. "And I'm sorry for bringing this danger to the ranch."

Gabriel stared at her, the muscles in his jaw battling each other. He seemed to be ready to start that tirade that was bubbling inside him, but he reached out, pulled Lauren to him and kissed the top of her head. It would have been a perfect moment if Lauren hadn't winced. It wasn't from the kiss, though. It was because of the pressure the hug was putting on her injured arm.

She stepped back, both her and Gabriel's gazes going to the fresh bandage, and Cameron figured Gabriel would have cursed if it hadn't been for the little ears in the room.

"You should have come to me when the trouble started," Gabriel insisted.

Lauren shook her head. "I thought the men who did this were cops."

"They weren't," Gabriel said without hesitation. "And I don't need ID's on them to know that."

Jameson made a sound of agreement, went to the babies and sank down on the floor next to them. "The one who accused you of hiring him had a prison tat on his neck. Plus, this wasn't the kind of attack a cop would do. Not a smart cop anyway. If they'd been the real deal, they could have gone to your house, flashed their badges and gained entry that way. You're the daughter and sister of cops, and you would have let them in."

Now it was Lauren who made a sound of agreement after making a soft moan. "I panicked. I didn't want them to get to Patrick."

Gabriel nodded. "Panicking is exactly what they wanted you to do because it caused you to run."

Her brother hadn't come out and said it, but he likely believed that it'd caused Lauren to run to the wrong man—Cameron. In Gabriel's way of thinking, she should have gone to him, immediately, and that way he could have perhaps prevented this attack.

"So, how did this baby swap happen?" Jameson asked.

It was the question that had been repeating through Cameron's mind. "Gilly maybe orchestrated it," he admitted.

Gabriel looked ready to mumble some more profanity, but he bit it off when he glanced at the boys. "To protect her son from Evelyn and that scumbag boyfriend of hers."

Cameron hated that his sister had been in a position like that, and he also hated he hadn't been there to give her another option.

"We need to start from the beginning," Gabriel continued a moment later. "We'll need DNA tests on the boys—"

"I've already done one on Patrick," Lauren volunteered. "I'm waiting on the results now."

"Good. But we have to do Isaac's, as well, and we should repeat Patrick's, too, and compare it to Cameron's." Gabriel looked at Cameron as if questioning to see if he was opposed to that. He wasn't. What Cameron was opposed to, though, was the fallout.

"I love Isaac," Cameron admitted. He hadn't intended to say that aloud. It was stating the obvious, and that *obvious* was true for Lauren, too. She loved Patrick.

Gabriel didn't need for them to spell out where this would eventually lead. To some kind of custody issues. Maybe a huge legal battle if Lauren tried to go after both boys.

"If the DNA results prove there was a switch," Gabriel went on, "then the next step will be to get hospital surveillance footage to see if we can spot who's responsible. In the meantime, I can get someone to the jail to question Evelyn."

"I can do that," Jameson volunteered, and he stood, taking his cell from his pocket. He was about to make a call, but the ringing shot through the room. Not Jameson's phone, though, but Lauren's.

She looked at her phone screen as if steeling herself up for what she might see there. Probably because she thought this could be another attacker. But she didn't look afraid. She groaned, a sound of frustration.

"It's Julia," she explained. "My late husband's sister."

Good. While it was obvious Lauren didn't want to talk to the woman, Cameron wanted to hear what she had to say. Especially since Julia could be a suspect in this. Of course, the most obvious person was Evelyn, and it didn't matter if she was locked up. People could do all sorts of bad things from behind bars.

"She calls you often?" Cameron asked.

"Rarely. And it's never a pleasant conversation. We talk mainly through our lawyers these days."

Lauren stepped out of the room, but Cameron followed her. Anything that happened right now could be related to the investigation, and he wanted to hear what Lauren's sister-in-law had to say. Lauren obliged by putting the call on speaker. She also moved as far up the hall as she could go.

"What the hell is going on?" Julia immediately demanded. No wonder Lauren had been dreading this. The woman was clearly hostile.

"I was about to ask you the same thing," Lauren countered without even pausing. "Someone tried to kill me, and I need to know if you had anything to do with that?"

"What? You'd better not be accusing me of something like that."

Cameron considered holding his tongue but then decided against it. "Lauren is fine, by the way. Good of you to ask."

"I don't care if she's fine," Julia spat out. "And who the hell are you anyway?"

"Deputy Cameron Doran," Lauren answered. If she was bothered by Cameron inserting himself into this conversation, she didn't show it. She just gave another weary sigh.

"Your old boyfriend." Julia said that as if Cameron were some kind of disease. "Yes, I know about you. I know everything about Lauren. She moaned out your name when she was under anesthesia after having an emergency appendectomy. *Cameron, Cameron,* she kept saying, so I did an internet search and found out you were a deputy in that hick town she comes from."

Cameron wasn't sure how to respond to that especially since the color began to rise in Lauren's cheeks. Maybe she hadn't wanted him to know that she'd thought about him over the years. It didn't mean anything, though. People in pain said all sorts of things that just happened to fall from their memories.

"Well, Deputy, are you the reason I had two cops at my house last night?" Julia demanded.

Cameron glanced at Lauren to see if she knew anything about that, but she only shook her head. "What cops?" Cameron pressed.

"How the heck should I know? Guys with badges. I saw them on the security camera outside my house and didn't answer the door. That's because I figured Lauren had sent them."

Lauren huffed. "And why would I do that?"

"To upset me. To try to intimidate me into backing off from the lawsuit. But guess what? I'm not backing off. *Ever.* My brother and I built his company— together. You didn't have anything to do with that. And it should be mine."

"Obviously Alden didn't agree with that because he left the company to Patrick."

Julia cursed, and it was pretty raw. "Because he didn't have time to change his will before he died. You saw to that, I'm sure. Always bad-mouthing me to him."

"I didn't need to bad-mouth you." Unlike Julia, Lauren's voice was practically calm. "Alden knew what you were."

Julia's profanity got even worse. The woman had a temper, and even though Cameron didn't need any more incentive for her to be a suspect, that only made him realize he needed to start digging into Julia's financials.

"Alden was stupid," Julia went on. "You had him eating right out of your hand. Hell, the kid doesn't even look like him, and yet he was willing to hand over a fortune to him."

Everything inside Cameron went still, and he reached out and muted the call for a moment. "Does Julia know about the baby swap?"

"No." But then Lauren shook her head again. "At least she's never given me any indication that she knew."

Well, that comment was definitely some kind of *indication*.

Cameron unmuted the phone. "Did you hire gunmen to come after Lauren?" he came out and asked the woman.

"I'm not going to dignify that with a response. Just tell her to quit sending cops to my house."

"I didn't send them," Lauren insisted, but she was talking to the air because Julia launched into another verbal tirade.

"No one else would have had a reason to send them. It had to be you."

"They might not have been cops," Cameron interrupted. "The men who tried to kill Lauren pretended to be police officers. Your visitors could have come to your house to kill you."

Julia gasped. "Why?"

"I don't know," Cameron answered. "Maybe for

the same reason they attacked Lauren. You said you saw the men on your security camera. Do you have footage we can study to see if we can try to identify them?"

"Maybe. I'll look." But she made it sound as if it'd be some big inconvenience. "Have you asked Duane if he has footage?"

Again, Lauren looked puzzled enough by Julia's comment that Cameron knew she was hearing this for the first time.

"Duane?" he questioned. Of course, Cameron had already heard the man's name. He was Alden's business partner, but he wasn't sure how the guy fit into this. Or even if he did fit.

"Duane Tulley," Julia snapped. "He called me about a half hour ago and said cops came to his house, too. He wasn't there. He was staying overnight with his girlfriend, but he has a remote security system and saw the men on the camera."

"Was it the same men who came to your place?" Cameron asked.

"Who knows. Maybe. Lauren, so help me, you'd better not be behind this."

"I'm not—" But that was all Lauren managed to say before Julia continued.

"Just keep me out of your problems. The lawsuit is going before a judge next month, and I don't want you playing games to try to sway this to your side."

Cameron was certain he looked just as puzzled

as Lauren did. "You think I'd fake an attack to get sympathy from a judge?"

"Yes, I do." And with that, Julia ended the call.

Lauren stared at the phone for a moment before she gave a heavy sigh and slid it back into her pocket. "Now you know why I thought Julia could be behind this. My sister-in-law hates me."

No way could Cameron argue with that. "Just how much money is at stake in Alden's estate?"

"At least twenty million."

Well, hell. That was plenty of motive for Julia to do all sorts of things. Including hiring someone to murder Lauren. That would definitely get Lauren out of the way and would give Julia control not just of the money but Patrick, as well.

Or rather, Isaac.

It twisted his insides to think of that woman having any kind of claim on the baby Cameron loved.

"I'll have to speak to Duane," Cameron told her. "I not only need the security tapes but I'll also need to question him." Julia, too, of course. "I'm guessing Duane has motive for wanting you dead?"

Lauren nodded, pushed her hair from her face. "It all goes back to the money. But if he could get Julia, Patrick and me out of the picture, Duane would inherit everything."

Cameron could see how that might play out. And that was playing out in a very bad way. "Duane could have hired those men to kill you with plans to set up

Julia. Then he could use DNA proof to verify that Patrick isn't Alden's son."

He watched as Lauren processed that and saw the exact moment she followed that through to what could happen next.

Duane would need to make Isaac disappear.

Because Isaac could indeed be Alden's rightful heir.

Hell, he needed to bring Duane in ASAP, too. But first he had to work on making sure Lauren and the babies were safe.

"I'm sorry," Lauren said, drawing his attention back to her.

The apology irritated him since this wasn't her fault. Well, for the most part anyway. Gabriel was right that she should have gone to him when this had first started, but she certainly didn't need to be feeling any regret about that.

She blinked hard, obviously still fighting those tears, and Cameron had to do some fighting of his own. He wanted to pull her into his arms, to try to reassure her that all would be well. But it was best not to break down the barriers Lauren had put up when she'd left town. Besides, he wasn't ready to forgive himself, either, for letting Travis walk that night of the murders.

"Yes," she said as if she knew exactly what he was thinking.

Lauren touched his arm, rubbed gently and then headed back toward the nursery. However, she didn't make it far before they spotted Jameson coming out of the room. He had a troubled look on his face.

Hell. What now?

"There could be a problem, and you both need to come back to the nursery," Jameson told them.

That got Lauren and Cameron moving plenty fast, but when they hurried into the room, the babies were fine. They were still playing on the floor, and the nannies were there with them. It looked like nothing was wrong.

Until he made eye contact with Merilee.

Cameron saw the fear again. The concern in Gabriel's expression, too.

"Evelyn's out of jail," Gabriel said. "And one of the hands just spotted her on the road that leads to your house."

Chapter Six

If someone had told Lauren two days ago that she'd be back at Gabriel's, she wouldn't have believed them. Yet, here she was. And not only was she dealing with the old memories of the murders, but she also had some new nightmares to add to the mix.

How was she going to keep the babies safe?

Gabriel had certainly done his part to make sure that happened. They'd moved both boys, the nannies, Cameron and her to his place. He'd assured her that he had a solid security system and that the hands would be patrolling the grounds. But Lauren wasn't sure that would be enough.

Especially with Evelyn out of jail.

Even though one of the hands had seen her near the ranch, she hadn't come to Cameron's or Gabriel's. Maybe because there had been cops and CSIs to scare her off. If she'd been the one behind the attack, she might not have realized all her hired guns had been killed, and she had possibly come with the hopes of snatching Isaac. Thankfully, that hadn't happened, but before Gabriel could get out to the road, the woman hadn't been there, either.

In fact, they didn't know where Evelyn was.

And that only added to Lauren's nightmarish thoughts.

She heard the footsteps outside the makeshift nursery that Gabriel and his wife, Jodi, had set up, and she reached for her gun. Which she no longer had. She'd put it on the top of the fridge because she didn't like the idea of having it on her when she was around the babies. But there was no reason for a gun anyway.

Because it was Cameron.

Like her, he'd spent most of the past two hours in the nursery, only stepping out to take calls. Lauren figured she should be making calls, as well, but she hadn't been able to tear herself away.

"They're still sleeping," Cameron whispered when his attention landed on the quilt where both boys were sacked out.

Hopefully, Dara was getting some rest in one of the guest rooms, as well. Merilee certainly was. She was napping on the daybed not far from the boys. With the high-stress day that they'd all had, Lauren figured the women were having a serious adrenaline crash. She certainly was and felt dead on her feet.

Cameron looked as exhausted as she did, and like her, he was probably having some pain. They'd declined the meds the medics had left for them, though.

No way did she want her mind clouded any more than it already was.

"Anything on Evelyn?" She, too, kept her voice at a whisper even though the boys hadn't stirred even when there'd been other noises in the house.

He kept his attention fixed on the boys but shook his head. "But she's definitely out of jail. She was released on parole two days ago, and the board didn't bother to contact me to let me know."

Two days. Enough time to orchestrate all of this. But something about that wasn't right.

"If Evelyn was behind this, why come after Patrick and me?" Lauren asked.

"Maybe because she found out about the baby switch." Cameron answered so quickly that it meant he'd given this some thought. "If she knew Patrick was her grandson, she'd do anything to get him."

Yes. But Lauren was still having trouble thinking of Patrick as anything but her child. He wasn't. He was Gilly's biological son, and that meant Evelyn could have some kind of legal claim to him.

That thought nearly brought her to her knees.

Lauren staggered a little, catching on to the door frame to steady herself. Cameron also caught on to her by slipping his arm around her.

"You can't let this get to you," he said, maybe figuring out what she'd just realized. "Evelyn has a police record. No judge is going to give her custody."

"No clean judge. But Evelyn certainly has the

money to pay one off. And hire as many fake cops and thugs as she wants."

The woman was a millionaire many times over, and that was probably why she hadn't spent much time in jail for pulling a gun on a cop. Still...

"If Evelyn wants her grandson so much, then why would she have put Patrick in danger like that?" she pressed.

He lifted his shoulder, and because he still had hold of her, it meant his arm slid against the side of her breast. He noticed, too, mumbled an apology and then eased away from her.

Lauren immediately felt the loss of no longer having him to support her. But it was a loss she shouldn't be feeling. She couldn't take that kind of comfort from Cameron. Not with this fire still simmering between them. A fire he was feeling, as well, she realized when their gazes connected.

He looked away from her, mumbled some profanity and then scrubbed his hand over his face. "Did you ever meet Evelyn?"

It was a good question, but she suspected he was asking to make sure they got their minds off that fire and back where it belonged—on figuring out who was behind the attacks.

"I met her once," Lauren answered. "It was at Gilly's apartment. I was there visiting your sister, and Evelyn showed up. Gilly wasn't pleased, and it wasn't a pleasant conversation. She wanted Gilly to have an amniocentesis done to prove the baby was her grandchild. Gilly refused. The test has risks, and there was no doubt in Gilly's mind that the baby was Trace's."

That gave her another jolt. Because the baby Gilly had been carrying had been Patrick.

"How did Gilly and you reconnect after you left Blue River?" he asked.

Lauren didn't have to think hard to remember that. "Gilly just rang my doorbell one day. She said she'd found me through an internet search and that she was moving to Dallas. We were both pregnant at the time, and she'd heard about my husband dying." Lauren paused. "Did Gilly tell you she'd moved near me?"

"No." His jaw tightened a little. "In fact, she didn't mention you at all. I knew you were in Dallas. That came up once when Gabriel was trying to get in touch with you."

Yes, Gabriel had tried many times. And early on after she'd left, Gabriel had come to see her every other month or so. There'd been nothing recent, though. Maybe he'd given up on ever bringing her back to the ranch. Ironic that it was danger and not family that had caused her to return.

"You knew Gilly was afraid of Trace?" Cameron continued a moment later.

She nodded. "I think Gilly might have moved to Dallas because it was far away from Trace but close to me. I don't believe she wanted to go through the pregnancy alone, and before my parents' murders, Gilly and I had been close."

Not that she needed to tell Cameron about that. He knew she'd been best friends with his sister because Lauren had spent plenty of time at their house. His folks were no longer around, though. His mom had died when Cameron was only six, and his dad had left shortly after Cameron became a deputy. It hadn't been a huge loss for Cameron or Gilly since their father had spent more time drinking than being a dad. Lauren supposed his father felt Gilly would be in good hands so Cameron had ended up raising his sister.

And now he was raising her son.

Or so Cameron had thought.

Lauren took a deep breath, ready to bring up the subject of what they were going to do, but from the corner of her eye, she spotted Jameson making his way toward them. He was sporting the same serious expression that he'd had since her arrival.

"You have a visitor," Jameson said, motioning toward the front of the house. "Duane Tully. He says it's important."

Cameron groaned. "He's not inside, is he?"

Jameson lifted his eyebrow in a "no-way" expression. "He's parked in the driveway with two hands watching him to make sure he stays put. I told him if it's really that important, he should head straight to the sheriff's office. He's still one of our suspects, right?"

"He has motive to kill me," Lauren verified. "Why does he want to see me?"

"He won't say. That makes me want to arrest him and haul him to jail."

Lauren wouldn't mind the man being in jail, but right now Duane seemed the "safest" of their suspects. As far as she knew, he'd never been in jail, never pulled a gun on a cop and wasn't brimming with venom the way Julia was.

"Gabriel was going to question Duane anyway," Cameron pointed out. "And I'd want to listen to what he has to say. I'd rather not have to leave Lauren and the boys right now to do that. So maybe Gabriel can question him here? After Duane is searched for weapons, that is."

Lauren didn't like the idea of being under the same roof as the man, but it was better than the alternative. Plus, they needed to ask him about the so-called cops that'd come to his house.

"Merilee," Cameron said the moment Jameson gave them the go-ahead nod.

The nanny's eyes immediately flew open, and she sprang to a sitting position. "What's wrong?"

"Maybe nothing," Cameron assured her. "I just need you to watch the babies while Lauren and I have a chat with someone."

Cameron waited until Merilee had gotten to her feet before he shut the door. Good. Isaac would probably nap for at least another half hour, and he would be cranky if he didn't get those extra minutes.

They went downstairs where Gabriel was waiting in the foyer. "You're seeing him?" he asked right off.

Lauren nodded.

Gabriel huffed. The kind of huff to indicate he wasn't sure this was the right thing to do. Lauren wasn't sure of that, either. But she did want to hear what Duane had to say. Besides, the house was as safe as the sheriff's office would be. Lauren could see armed ranch hands outside, and Jodi was at the front window—her gun drawn. She would no doubt watch to make sure Duane hadn't brought any hired guns with him, and since Jodi was a security specialist, she had nearly as much training as Gabriel.

"I'll frisk him," Gabriel grumbled. He glanced at his wife, a stay-safe warning passing between them, before he headed out.

When Gabriel opened the door, Cameron automatically pulled Lauren behind him, and Jameson stepped in front of her, as well. Again, they were risking their lives for her, and she hated that it'd come down to that. However, despite their quick maneuvering, she still managed to get a glimpse of Duane.

And he got a glimpse of her, too. Duane looked weary and not at all there to do battle with her. That was something, at least. Considering he'd filed a lawsuit against her for Alden's estate, she didn't expect him to be friendly, but maybe he could give them something to help with the investigation.

"Ivy called a little while ago," Jameson told her as they waited for Gabriel.

Ivy, her sister. Like plenty of other things about being at the ranch, her sister's name brought back more of those old memories. Mostly good. Once, Ivy and she had been close. But like Lauren, Ivy hadn't stayed in Blue River, either. She'd left shortly after the murders and had only recently come home.

"Ivy wants to see you," Jameson went on. "Theo and she are down in Houston clearing out her place there, but I told them that for now they should stay put."

Good. Lauren wanted to see her sister, as well, but it was too risky for Ivy to be here since she also had a son. There were already enough people in danger at the ranch.

"I'm sure you remember Theo," Jameson added. "Well, Ivy and he are engaged now."

That created some sudden tension in the foyer. Not because Ivy and Theo were back together. That didn't surprise Lauren. The two had always been in love. But Theo's father, Travis, was in jail for murdering Lauren's parents. Obviously, her sister had gotten past that if she was planning to marry Theo.

Lauren hadn't quite managed to do that, though. And that lack of getting over it involved Cameron. He didn't say anything—he didn't need to—but it was always there. Because he was the lone person who'd had the chance to stop Travis that horrible night, and he hadn't done it. One day Lauren would ask her sister how she'd put that all behind her, and then maybe she could do the same.

Jameson adjusted his stance again, and both Cameron and he slid their hands over their guns as Gabriel approached the house. He had his hand clamped around Duane's arm as if arresting the man.

"Lauren," Duane greeted. The moment he was inside, Gabriel shut the door and armed the security alarm.

Yes, the stress was definitely there, etched around Duane's eyes, and he wasn't the polished businessman that he usually was. He was wearing jeans and a casual shirt rather than the pricey suits that he favored.

"I heard about the attack from Julia," Duane said to her. "I came as soon as I could."

Lauren shook her head. "How'd you get here so fast?" His house was hours away in Dallas.

"I was already on my way. I wanted to talk to you after those cops showed up at my house last night. Julia said you sent them to harass me, but I figured there was more to it than that."

"I didn't send them," Lauren insisted. "And I have reason to believe they could have been hired killers."

"Yes, the sheriff mentioned that to me. You really think someone would want me dead?"

"I don't know," she answered honestly. "I also don't know who hired the men or why they came after me. But you should take precautions just in case."

Duane looked at all three lawmen, maybe to see if they agreed with that, and even though Cameron,

Gabriel and Jameson didn't speak, Duane must have seen something on their faces to make him nod.

"I'll look into hiring a bodyguard." He took a piece of paper from his pocket and handed it to Gabriel. "That's the code to access the online storage for the footage from my security system. Maybe you can compare the faces of the men who came to my door to the ones who were killed here at the ranch."

Lauren hoped she was wrong, but the way Duane had said that last part almost made it seem as if he was sympathetic about the thugs who'd attacked them and been shot in the process.

"What about Julia?" Cameron asked Gabriel. "Has she turned over her footage?"

"Not yet." Gabriel looked at the paper and then went into the adjoining living room to use a laptop that was on the coffee table. Jodi stayed at the window, keeping watch.

"Don't expect Julia to just cooperate," Duane muttered. He made a sound of frustration. "Julia's the reason I wanted to come and talk to you face-to-face," he added to Lauren. But he didn't say anything else. He just stood there, glancing around as if trying to figure out what to do.

"Did Julia do something I should know about?" Lauren came out and asked. "Did she hire those men?"

"I honestly don't have any idea about that." Duane paused again. "But I do know she's getting desperate. Did you know she's practically broke?"

Lauren hadn't thought Duane could say anything that would surprise her, but she'd obviously been wrong. "No. And that doesn't sound right. Both Alden and Julia inherited huge trust funds—"

"Julia drained hers to pay off some bad investments," Duane interrupted. "She doesn't want anyone to know," he quickly added, "but a PI I hired learned about it when I had him looking into some background stuff for the lawsuit."

Since Duane had filed that lawsuit against Lauren, she very much wanted to hear this—and especially why he'd included Julia in it.

"How and what did the PI learn?" Cameron asked, taking the words right out of Lauren's mouth.

Duane glanced away from her again. Not a good sign.

"I was looking for something to prove you cheated on Alden," the man finally said. "Yes, I know it's a stretch, but I can't just hand over the company that I helped build."

"You're not handing it over. You still own twenty-five percent. As does Julia."

"And Patrick owns the rest, the majority share," Duane spelled out for her. "You know that Alden wanted me to run the company."

"I know no such thing," Lauren argued. "In fact, at the time of Alden's death, you two were at odds with each other. He didn't approve of some of the investments you'd made. Were they bad investments like Julia's?"

"No," Duane snapped, and he repeated it. "It was just a difference of opinion, something Alden and I would have worked out if he'd lived."

He stared at her as if waiting for her to say something. Maybe something about giving in to him and handing over Patrick's shares. But they weren't hers to give.

Heck, they weren't even Patrick's.

They were Isaac's.

If Duane knew that, he might be trying to get rid of the baby so he'd have a better shot at getting the company. Of course, Julia had an equal motive since she wanted her hands on the money from Alden's estate.

"Alden was my best friend," Duane went on, "and while you and I never really got along, I don't want to see his son harmed."

Lauren pulled back her shoulders so fast that it caused her stitches to pull, and the pain rippled through her. Cameron noticed, too, because he leaned in and made brief eye contact with her before his attention slashed to Duane.

"Explain that," Cameron demanded. "Who would want to harm his son?"

"Julia." This time Duane didn't hesitate. "The PI I hired not only learned she was nearly broke, but he also found out she's in debt to a loan shark. I think she's past being desperate and would do anything to get her hands on her brother's money.

"And the only way Julia could do that would be

to kill Patrick and her. If Julia knew there was a possibility of a baby swap, then that could send her after Isaac, too.

"I know about the DNA test you had done on your son," Duane added. "Yes, I know it's snooping, but I'm desperate, too. Not like Julia, but I want to hang on to my company."

Cameron glanced at her, no doubt to see if she was aware that Duane knew about the test, and she wasn't.

"What DNA test?" Lauren asked. Yes, it was a lie for her to pretend she didn't know what he was talking about, but she didn't intend to confirm anything to Duane.

"The PI had someone follow you," Duane admitted. "He saw you go to the lab. He went in after you when the receptionist was logging in the information."

Sweet heaven. If the PI had found out about that, then Julia could have, too. In fact, it was possible that Julia had had someone watching her, as well.

"The DNA test was for me," Lauren said. Again, it was a lie. "There were rumors my mother had had an affair, and I wanted to be sure that Sherman Beckett was really my father."

Duane couldn't have possibly looked more skeptical. Probably because Jameson and she were side by side, and the resemblance was definitely there. However, Duane hadn't known her folks so maybe he would think they resembled their mother.

"I'll have to send the footage to the crime lab for confirmation," Gabriel said, coming back into the foyer. "But I'm pretty sure the men who paid you a visit are the same ones who tried to kill us."

Some of the color drained from Duane's face. "Julia," he said through clenched teeth. "You have to stop her. Arrest her. Get her to confess."

"Give us everything your PI found out about her," Cameron fired back, "and maybe that'll be enough to get a warrant."

Maybe. Without proof, it would be just hearsay, but it was possible the PI had found something else.

Duane turned as if to leave, but he stopped and made eye contact with Lauren again. "The best way to stop Julia might be to settle the lawsuit with her. That could give her the money to pay the loan shark, and she might back off."

That was true if Julia was the one behind this. But Alden hadn't wanted his sister to have the money, and again, it wasn't Lauren's to give away. Still, it was something to consider if it would keep the babies out of danger.

"I suppose you want Lauren to settle the lawsuit with you, too," Cameron commented to Duane.

Duane shrugged, the answer obvious. "All I'm asking for is enough of the shares so I'll be majority holder. Her son can keep the rest. And it's only fair since it's my company."

That set her teeth on edge because it wasn't only his. And again, she didn't want to barter off Isaac's birthright. One day he might want to run his father's company. It would be easier for Lauren to give up the money since she had plenty of her own that she could pass onto her children, but if she gave Duane the company, she would never be able to get it back.

"I'll think about that and let you know what I decide," she settled for saying.

She expected Duane to look at least slightly optimistic about that. He didn't. He studied her expression as if trying to figure out if she would truly consider it, and then he mumbled something she didn't catch. Lauren didn't believe it was a compliment, though.

With a scowl on his face, Duane motioned for Gabriel to disarm the security system. Her brother did, and he closed the door behind the man. Gabriel also stood at the side windows, no doubt to make sure Duane left.

"Lawsuits?" Jameson repeated.

Lauren nodded. "Both Julia and Duane are suing me. Well, suing Patrick anyway." She paused. "If I can prove a baby swap, then the lawsuits will have to be refiled. That'll cause delays that neither Duane nor Julia will like."

"No," Cameron agreed.

Cameron didn't spell it out, but Lauren figured they were thinking the same thing. That it would be easier for Julia or Duane to eliminate Isaac. Or maybe even both boys.

"You believe what Duane said about Julia owing money to a loan shark?" Gabriel asked.

Lauren had to shrug. "I suppose it could be true. Alden always claimed Julia was irresponsible with money. That's one of the main reasons he didn't want to turn over any part of his estate to her. That, and he wanted Patrick…his son…to have it."

But if it was true about Julia's debts, then that made her even more dangerous.

"I'll get Julia in for questioning," Gabriel assured her.

She was about to tell Cameron and her brothers that they needed to do more to beef up security and they had to make sure neither Duane nor Julia got anywhere near the babies, but Cameron's phone rang before she could speak.

"It's Jace Morrelli," Cameron relayed when he looked at the screen.

Since Jace was another of Gabriel's deputies, that immediately snagged her attention. He could have updates on the investigation, and thankfully Cameron put the call on speaker so she could listen.

"Evelyn Waters just showed up here at the sheriff's office," Jace said without a greeting. "She's demanding to see Lauren and you."

"Is she armed?" Gabriel asked right off. "If she is, arrest her because it'll be a violation of her parole."

"I searched her. No weapons. But she's talking crazy. That's why I called you." It sounded as if Jace blew out a long breath. "She's claiming that Lauren swapped her baby with Gilly's, and Evelyn insists she can prove it."

Chapter Seven

Cameron wasn't sure if this was the right thing to do—bringing Lauren to the sheriff's office. But he'd figured since Evelyn was there and making wild accusations, then Gabriel and he might as well do an interview with not only her but Julia, as well.

Neither conversation would be pleasant.

Still, they were necessary. What wasn't necessary was for Lauren to be there, but she had insisted. Well, she had after Gabriel had assigned two deputies to guard the babies. With Jameson, Jodi and the hands there, as well, Cameron hoped it was enough protection so that hired thugs couldn't get to them.

"You can't go into the interview room," Cameron reminded Lauren when Gabriel pulled to a stop in front of the sheriff's office.

"I'm still going to talk to Evelyn," she insisted. "I want to know how she found out about the baby swap. And why she thinks I'm responsible for it."

Cameron could only sigh. She wanted to confront the woman—he got that—but Lauren had already been through hell and back, and Evelyn wasn't going to make this situation better. Even with that, Cameron doubted he could have stopped Lauren if he'd tried. If he'd been in her shoes, he would have wanted the same thing.

He opened the cruiser door, taking hold of Lauren's hand so he could get her inside as fast as possible. Gabriel did the same. Cameron had hoped they'd have a moment before they had to face the storm, but the "storm" was right there. Evelyn was in the squad room, seated next to Jace's desk, and she stood the moment she laid eyes on them.

Cameron hadn't thought that jail time would ease the hatred Evelyn had for him, and it hadn't. He could see plenty of it in her eyes, but this time the hatred wasn't just for him. No. The woman was aiming some of it at Lauren, too.

"You swapped the babies, didn't you?" Evelyn said, the emotion causing her voice to tremble.

Lauren shook her head. "I don't know what you mean. What swap?"

"You know. You damn well know," Evelyn snapped.

"Uh, you want me to hang around or should I get the interview room ready?" Gabriel asked.

"Definitely get the room ready," Cameron assured him. "Evelyn obviously has a lot to say." Maybe she'd say the wrong thing and implicate herself in the attacks.

Mumbling some profanity under his breath, Gabriel went toward the hall, where there were a pair of interview rooms and his office.

"I do have plenty to say," Evelyn verified. "Plenty to tell you about my grandson being swapped with Lauren's baby."

"Why would I do something like that?" Lauren fired right back at her.

"To keep Trace's son from me, that's why." She shifted her attention to Cameron. "How long have you known and why didn't you tell me?" Evelyn's voice had gotten louder with each word.

"A reminder," Cameron warned her. "You're on probation. Keep your temper in check, or I will put you back in jail."

She stood there as if daring him to try that, and part of him wanted her to push this so he could lock her back up. Then she might not be a threat to the boys. But first he wanted Evelyn to explain some things.

"Why do you believe someone switched the babies?" Cameron asked.

Evelyn huffed as if the answer was obvious. And maybe it was. Maybe she'd seen a picture of Patrick. The boy didn't look like Trace, but he did resemble the Dorans.

"I got a phone call two days ago," Evelyn said. "The person didn't identify himself, but he said Lauren had done a DNA test on her baby, and the reason she'd done that was because he wasn't hers. He was Trace's."

Now it was Lauren's turn to sigh because she hadn't missed the timing of this. It was when the PI Duane hired had followed Lauren to the lab. Apparently, Cameron needed to have another chat with the man to find out why he'd involved Evelyn in this.

"The DNA test was for me," Lauren said, repeating the lie she'd told Duane. "There was some question about whether or not Sherman Beckett was actually my father."

Like Duane, Evelyn didn't seem to buy that, either. "After I got that call," Evelyn went on, "I did some digging. I found the names of the staff who were working for those three days that both boys were in the hospital nursery."

Since the other deputies were working on the same thing, that piqued Cameron's interest. "And?"

"Dr. Gina Boyer," Evelyn said without hesitation. "I don't have the proof yet, but it all points to her."

Cameron looked at Lauren to see if she recognized the name, and she nodded. "She was an OB resident."

"And in debt up to her eyeballs," Evelyn provided. "She transferred to another hospital less than a week after the babies were born."

Cameron took a notepad from Jace's desk, jotted down the doctor's name and handed it to his fellow deputy. "Find out everything you can about her."

Jace nodded and got right on that, and Cameron turned back to Evelyn. "Did you contact this doctor?"

"I tried. She wouldn't take my calls. Wouldn't see me, either. That alone is suspicious."

"Maybe." Cameron shrugged. "Or maybe she's just busy and didn't want to talk to a stranger."

Evelyn's mouth tightened. "She wouldn't talk to me because she knows I'm onto her. She knows that I found out Lauren paid her to switch the babies."

A weary sigh left Lauren's mouth. "Again, why would I possibly do that?"

"Because of that barracuda of a sister-in-law, Julia. You must have known it would make your boy a target so you decided to make my grandson a target instead."

Since Cameron's arm was against hers, he felt her muscles tense. "I would have never done that," Lauren insisted, but her voice was now a tight whisper.

"No?" It didn't sound as if Evelyn was buying that, either. "Then who switched them?"

"I don't have any proof anyone did," Lauren answered. "And apparently neither do you. Now I have a question for you—did you hire thugs to attack me?"

Evelyn huffed. "Right. Go ahead. Try to wiggle out of this by putting the blame on me."

"You have a history of violent behavior," Cameron reminded the woman. A reminder that earned him a glare.

"I pulled a gun on you because I was desperate." She had to say that through clenched teeth. "Because you wouldn't let me see my grandson. Now I find out he wasn't my blood, after all."

"Does that mean you're about to accuse me of swapping the boys?" he pressed when the woman didn't continue.

Evelyn's eyes narrowed as if she might be considering that, but she shook her head. "I don't think you knew. But she did." She tipped her head to Lauren. "And now that psycho sister-in-law is coming after her."

Cameron's hands went on his hips. "That's your second reference to Julia. How do you know her?"

"I don't. Never met the woman. But I don't have to know her to have her investigated. After I got that phone call about the DNA test, I had my staff drop everything they were doing and start looking into things."

Since Evelyn owned a large public relations firm, she probably did have the manpower to dig up plenty of dirt, but it made him wonder if all of this was meant to cast blame on Julia or even Lauren so the blame wouldn't be squarely on her own shoulders. Yes, Julia and Duane had motives. But so did Evelyn.

Gabriel reappeared in the hall and motioned for Evelyn to follow him. She did. And Cameron and Lauren were about to do the same, but Jace stopped them. He had the landline phone pressed to his ear and was holding his hand over the speaker part.

"I have Dr. Boyer on the line," Jace said once Evelyn was out of earshot. "You want to talk to her now?"

Cameron couldn't take the phone fast enough, and

he put it on speaker for Lauren. "Dr. Boyer, I'm Deputy Cameron Doran from the Blue River Sheriff's Office, and I have Lauren Lange with—"

"Yes, this is about that woman, Evelyn Waters," the doctor interrupted. "She's left more than a dozen messages on my work phone, and I believe she has someone following me."

Cameron didn't doubt that, and since it appeared the doctor knew what this was all about, he launched right into his question. "Evelyn believes you might have taken part in a baby swap that happened a year ago. Did you?"

"No," she answered.

He didn't like the doctor's hesitation or the fact that she didn't even add anything to that. In his experience, innocent people tended to protest a lot when accused of a crime. "Did you have contact with Gilly Doran's and Lauren's newborn sons?"

"Of course. I was working at the hospital when they were born. I was one of your sister's doctors and was with her when she died." Another hesitation. "She's the reason I left and went to another hospital. Gilly was one of my first patients. The first one I ever lost," Dr. Boyer added.

So, maybe she wasn't covering up anything and this was just a difficult conversation for her. It was certainly difficult for him. This doctor had been there with his sister, but he hadn't been. That was a wound that was never going to fully heal. Now he had to do what was right by Gilly and make sure her son was safe.

"Dr. Boyer, this is Lauren," she said. "I've had some trouble. Someone's been trying to kill me."

It sounded as if the doctor gasped. "You don't think that has anything to do with something that happened at the hospital?"

"I don't know. That's what we're trying to find out. My son and Gilly's son could be in danger, and you might be able to help."

The doctor certainly didn't jump to offer anything. Finally, though, she asked, "How?"

"Just think back to those two days that our babies were in the hospital nursery at the same time," Lauren continued. "Did Gilly say anything about her son being in danger? Or maybe you saw someone suspicious?"

"You mean someone like Evelyn Waters?"

Cameron saw Lauren go stiff. "Yes. Did you see her?"

"I can't be sure," the doctor said after a long pause. "It's possible. That was over a year ago, and I wasn't getting a lot of sleep. There were so many people in and out, and I didn't really even know the other staff yet."

That sounded like a perfect storm for someone wanting to do a baby swap. But if it'd been Evelyn, why hadn't she just tried to take the child?

If that was indeed her plan, that is.

There was another angle to this.

"Did my sister tell you about her abusive ex, the man who was the father of her child?" Cameron asked.

"Yes." The doc didn't sound so eager to admit to that. "She showed me a picture of him and begged me not to let him get near the baby."

Cameron was thankful for that, but he needed to know if the doctor had taken it past the stage of merely looking out for Trace.

"Did Gilly ever mention anything about swapping the babies to keep them from her ex?" Cameron pressed.

Silence.

The moments crawled by, causing Cameron to curse under his breath.

"No," Dr. Boyer finally answered. "Look, Deputy Doran, I have to go. A patient here needs me."

Before Cameron could say anything else, the doctor ended the call. Cameron stood there, staring at the phone and debating if he should try to call her back. But he doubted she would answer. Besides, he should do a background check on her and see what they were dealing with. First, though, he wanted to hear if Evelyn would give Gabriel anything they could use.

"I don't think Gilly could have done the swap on her own," Lauren said as they walked toward the observation room next to where the interview was taking place.

"If she was desperate enough, she could have figured out a way." Cameron silently cursed that, too.

His sister had been so desperate because he hadn't been there to help her.

"Don't put this on yourself." Lauren touched his arm and rubbed it gently.

Cameron didn't like that her touch gave him some comfort—her words, too—but it did. The comfort felt, well, nice, but he needed to focus on what Evelyn was saying. Except she wasn't saying what he wanted to hear.

"I think it's time I brought in my lawyer," he heard Evelyn say once Lauren and he were in the observation room.

Lauren groaned, and Gabriel looked as if he wanted to do the same. Cameron wasn't sure what'd caused the woman to play the lawyer card, but it meant this interview was over. Or at least it would be until Evelyn's attorney arrived. Thankfully, she took out her phone and made the call that would hopefully get him or her out here ASAP.

"And I'd like some coffee while I wait," Evelyn added when Gabriel stood.

Gabriel didn't agree to get her any, but he left the interview and came into the observation room with them.

"What happened?" Lauren immediately asked.

"I asked her if she had anything to do with those dead gunmen."

It was a question that needed to be asked so Cameron couldn't fault Gabriel for it. Still, this was a frustrating delay. "Did Evelyn say anything before she pulled the plug on the interview?"

"Not really. Just a rehash of what she said in the squad room."

Too bad. And Cameron wasn't going to be able to add anything in the good news department. "Lauren and I talked to Dr. Boyer. I think she's hiding something, so we need to get her in for questioning."

Gabriel gave a weary sigh, nodded and glanced at Evelyn through the mirror. The woman was taking out her phone. "I've got some calls to make so keep an eye on her. She might pitch a fit if she figures out I've locked the door, but I don't like a parolee being able to walk around in the place. Not with Lauren here anyway."

Cameron agreed. Evelyn herself wasn't that formidable, but she could be calling in another round of hired thugs. What they needed was to be able to find a money trail that linked Evelyn to the dead guys. Or to one of their other suspects. Right now all they had were a bunch of pieces and no way to put them together to tell them who was guilty.

"I hate to even bring it up," Lauren continued after Gabriel had left, "but is there any chance Travis Canton could be behind this?"

"You mean because of the threats we've all been getting," Cameron finished for her. "I doubt it." Now, this was something *he* hated to bring up. "Travis hasn't exactly been hostile to me, and he actually liked Gilly. I can't imagine him doing anything to put her boy in danger."

Of course, the man had been convicted of a double homicide so that meant he was pretty much capable of anything. "I'll check with the prison and make sure he hasn't had any unusual visitors," Cameron offered.

Lauren made a soft sound, part frustration, part groan. "This is why I hate being here in Blue River. It always comes back." She squeezed her eyes shut for a moment, and Cameron thought maybe she was fighting back tears again.

He was fighting back some regret. Not just for what he hadn't prevented that night ten years ago but for what he was about to do now. Even though he knew it wasn't a smart idea, Cameron glanced at Evelyn to make sure she had stayed put—she had—then he slipped his arm around Lauren and pulled her to him.

Just like that, time vanished, and they were suddenly lovers again. And it was something his body wasn't going to let him forget.

She leaned back, staying in his arms, but Lauren looked up at him. Yep, he'd been right about those tears. Her eyes were filled with them, and they were threatening to spill down her cheeks. He brushed his mouth over one when it fell.

Not a smart idea, either. But then he seemed to be going for broke in the "making huge mistakes" department. He cupped her chin, using his thumb to catch another tear. Of course, that meant touching her while the air was electric between them. Added to that, Lauren was definitely in vulnerable mode right now. That was probably why she didn't move away from him.

Cameron, however, couldn't explain why he didn't move away from her.

His feet seemed nailed to the floor. So he stood there, volleying glances at the mirror while waiting for either Lauren or him to put icing on this by going in for a kiss. He wanted that. Badly. Judging from the uneven rhythm of Lauren's breath, so did she. And for a couple of moments Cameron had no trouble remembering how her mouth would feel against his. How she would taste.

Since it was obvious neither of them had any sense left to do the right thing, fate got involved and helped them out. The sound of the footsteps, followed by someone clearing their throat, finally got them apart. Lauren practically scampered away from him. That probably had something to do with the fact that Gabriel was in the doorway, and he was scowling at them.

Cameron and he were friends, but that didn't mean Gabriel wanted him to get involved with Lauren again. Especially at a dangerous time like this. Added to that, Cameron really did need to keep his focus on the investigation.

"I just got off the phone with the lab," Gabriel

said, his scowl still in place. "The one that Lauren used to do Patrick's DNA."

Cameron felt his stomach tighten, and Lauren caught on to his arm as if to steady herself.

"It's not good," Gabriel added. "Someone stole the test results."

Chapter Eight

Lauren rocked Patrick in the chair in the nursery. Across from her, Merilee was doing the same thing to Isaac in another rocker that Cameron had brought over from his house.

Cameron wasn't in the room, though. Since they'd returned from the sheriff's office hours earlier, he was in the kitchen making calls and working the case. Something Lauren wanted to be doing, as well, but she didn't even know what else she could do. She'd called the lab immediately after Gabriel had told her the test results had been stolen, but she hadn't gotten much of an explanation.

Simply put, the lab tech didn't know what'd happened. According to him, he'd run the test, but when Gabriel had called to press him for the results, it wasn't there. Someone had deleted it from the computer log. Now Cameron was trying to figure out who'd done that since the same person was likely responsible for the attacks.

But why would someone want the results hidden?

Lauren didn't have an answer for that—though part of her wished there was some way for both boys to be biologically hers. Then she would have a claim on them. Of course, Cameron was perhaps wishing the same thing.

Eventually, they would have test results, though, since Gabriel had taken DNA not only from the boys but also from Cameron and her. Soon they would have confirmation of what Lauren already knew. No. It was more than that. She felt it all the way to her bones.

"It's funny how the boys are on the same schedule," Merilee whispered. She smiled down at Isaac. "They eat, nap and wake up around the same time." She got up and eased Isaac into the crib.

Lauren made a sound of agreement, and since Patrick was completely sacked out for his nap, she put him in the crib next to Isaac. Despite the nightmare that was going on, it soothed her to see them so peaceful like this.

"I'll be in the kitchen helping Dara with dinner," Merilee added. "Wouldn't be a good idea to rely on Cameron or Jodi to fix anything."

So Lauren had heard. Apparently, sandwich-making was the limit to their culinary skills. Lauren still had some baby food in the diaper bag she'd brought with her, but Dara had insisted on cooking something from scratch. Now the nanny was making the rest of them dinner.

Since the boys would likely sleep through the

night, Lauren took the baby monitor so she could find a quiet place to start making some calls to friends who might have heard something, anything, about Julia or Duane. Then she planned on sleeping in the nursery. It wouldn't be as comfortable as the guest room that Jodi had fixed up for her, but she didn't want to be far from the boys.

In case more of those hired guns tried to come after them again.

Gabriel probably wouldn't like it, but Lauren wanted to hire some extra security. Maybe some bodyguards. And that was going to be the first call she made. However, she'd barely had time to go into the hall when she saw Cameron making his way toward her.

He glanced in at the boys, then at the monitor she was holding before he motioned for her to follow him. He didn't go far, just into the foyer. The overhead light was on there. Unlike the nursery, where all the blinds and curtains had been closed all afternoon. Lauren had realized it was already dark outside.

When Cameron stopped and turned to her, he opened his mouth. Closed it. As if he'd changed his mind about what to say.

"Are you okay?" he asked.

Lauren didn't want to know how bad she looked for him to say that. Probably about as bad as she felt. "Just tired and frustrated."

"Yeah." She heard the frustration in his voice, too. But that wasn't only frustration in his eyes.

Maybe Cameron was remembering the near kiss that'd happened at the sheriff's office. Lauren hadn't thought for a minute that she was fully over Cameron, and that moment between them had proven it.

He glanced away as if knowing what she was thinking. "You want the good news or the bad news first?" he asked.

Lauren sighed. "The good." Since she wasn't ready for anything else bad, she figured she needed something—anything—positive first. And this attraction between them definitely didn't fall into the positive category.

"I found out more about Dr. Boyer," Cameron explained. "No red flags whatsoever. She left the hospital where the babies were born so she could move to Austin to be near her family. Her mom has late-stage cancer."

So the doctor hadn't fled after doing a baby switch. "But why did she sound, well, suspicious when she was talking to you?"

He lifted his shoulder. "My guess is that she got too close to Gilly, and she blamed herself in some way for Gilly's death."

The doctor shouldn't do that because Gilly had died from a blood clot. It wasn't common, but it did happen, and in Gilly's case, there was nothing anyone could have done to stop it.

Lauren took a deep breath and tried to steel herself up. "What's the bad news? And please don't tell me we're about to be attacked again."

"No attack. The hands are guarding the road and checking anyone coming in and out of the ranch. Jameson even has a couple of his Ranger friends helping."

Good. But she still wasn't nixing the idea of bodyguards just yet.

"Evelyn is making waves," Cameron said a moment later. "As soon as she left the sheriff's office, she had her team of lawyers petition a judge for custody of Patrick."

Lauren shook her head. "But she doesn't even have proof that Patrick is her son's baby."

"Oh, she's petitioning to get DNA results, too." He rubbed his hand over the back of his neck. "The thing is—Evelyn stands no chance of getting custody unless she can prove in some way that you or I hid her grandson from her. She'll want to make the judge believe we obstructed justice in some way."

Well, it definitely wasn't good news, but Lauren wasn't sure it was enough of a threat to put that troubled expression on Cameron's face. "There's no proof because we didn't do anything like that."

But then it hit her.

"While we're being investigated, a judge could put the babies in foster care." Just saying it aloud caused Lauren to stagger back, and she caught on to the wall.

"Isaac would be fine, probably," Cameron added. "Because a judge would likely give temporary custody of him to one of your siblings. But Evelyn and I are the only living relatives that Patrick has."

That nearly knocked the breath out of her and made Lauren even more unsteady. Cameron noticed, too, because he slid his arm around her. "They can't take Patrick. I won't let them."

"Neither will I," he assured her.

Cameron said that with such confidence that she looked up at him to make sure he wasn't lying. He wasn't. "He's my nephew, and I'll hide him if I have to."

He'd break the law—which no doubt would cut him to the core. But the cut would be even deeper if Patrick was taken away from her. She'd break plenty of laws to keep him. Of course, Evelyn and the law weren't her only threats.

Cameron was, too.

"What are we going to do?" Lauren came out and asked. "What are *you* going to do?" she amended.

He didn't ask her to clarify, but he did look as if he wanted to repeat the question to her. "I wish there was an easy fix for this."

So did she. But there wasn't, and it was breaking her heart. Cameron must have seen that, as well, because he said some profanity under his breath and pulled her to him. Lauren didn't resist. Nor did she stop herself from looking up at him. It was a mistake, of course, because they were already too close to each other. Especially their mouths. And that was never a good thing when it came to Cameron and her.

"I should go back into the kitchen," he said.

But he didn't, and Lauren didn't let go of him, either, so he could do that. Instead, she slipped her arm around his waist, drawing him even closer than he already was.

Cameron said more of that profanity before his mouth came to hers. The jolt was instant, a reminder of all those feelings and memories she'd been battling since she'd come back to the ranch. It was almost too much, and in some ways, it wasn't nearly enough.

Because it made her want more of him.

Cameron must have known that because he deepened the kiss, sliding his hand around the back of her neck and angling her so that she got an even stronger dose of those old feelings. New ones, as well. Cameron had always known how to set her body on fire, and he clearly hadn't forgotten that. But there was something different, too. The kind of intensity between two people who were no longer kids.

The stakes were sky-high, and that seemed to make the kiss even better. And worse. Worse because it was so good and made her wish that it wouldn't end with just a kiss.

However, it did end.

Cameron snapped away from her, and in the same motion, he pushed her behind him and drew his gun. Because the kiss had clouded her mind, it took Lauren a moment to realize why he'd done that. Because someone was out on the porch.

"It's one of the hands," Gabriel said.

Lauren also hadn't known that her brother was so close, and she wondered if he'd seen that kiss. If so, she was certain she would catch some flack about it later.

Lauren quickly looked out the window so she could see the ranch hand. She recognized him. Allen Colley. He'd started working for her family when she was a kid.

"Two San Antonio cops just showed up," Gabriel added. "Not alone, either. They have Julia with them."

Lauren immediately looked at her brother for an explanation, but Gabriel didn't give her one. "Step to the side," he instructed.

Lauren didn't want to do that. She wanted to see what was going on, but she did move into the adjoining living room. She wasn't in the direct line of the door, but she could still see from the window.

"The babies," she said, glancing down at the monitor.

"They'll be fine," Gabriel assured her. "These guys don't have a court order or search warrant so they're not getting in the house."

Good. But if they didn't have those things, then she wondered why Gabriel had allowed them onto the ranch.

Her brother disarmed the security system and opened the door. That was when Lauren spotted the SAPD cruiser parked in front of Gabriel's house. The two uniformed officers were already out of their vehicle, and Julia was between them.

"What do they want?" Cameron asked.

"Julia supposedly has some info that's critical to our investigation." Gabriel slid his hand over his gun, and that was when Lauren realized this could all be some kind of hoax. More fake cops. Ones that Julia herself could have hired.

"I checked with SAPD," Allen said, not looking any more comfortable about this than Gabriel, Cameron and she were. "The lieutenant confirmed these guys were his and that he'd sent them out here."

Lauren still wasn't breathing easier just yet because the lieutenant could be dirty, too. She hated that she could no longer trust everyone with a badge, but it was too risky to let down her guard.

"I'm Sergeant Terry Welker," the officer on the right greeted them. He was yet someone else who didn't look especially pleased about this visit. He tipped his head to the other cop. "This is Detective Miguel Rodriguez. I'm pretty sure you know Ms. Lange."

"They know me, all right, and they're trying to smear my name," Julia promptly snapped.

Cameron reholstered his gun and huffed. "It's not a smear if it's the truth. You're desperate for cash because you're in debt to a loan shark." He shifted his attention to the sergeant. "Did she tell you that?"

Julia certainly didn't jump to deny it, which meant she probably thought they had some kind of proof.

They didn't. Well, other than Duane's accusations, but since he was a suspect, too, Lauren wasn't about to accept everything he'd told them. But in this case, it appeared Duane had been right.

Lauren moved back to the edge of the foyer, coming into Julia's view. The woman aimed a scowl at her, but Lauren gave the woman one right back. Because owing money to a loan shark was plenty of motive for the attacks. It sickened Lauren to think the babies could be in danger because of money.

"This visit doesn't have anything to do with that," Julia insisted. "Believe it or not, I've come to help you. Not for your sakes. But so you'll leave me the hell alone."

Cameron didn't ask how she'd come to help. Instead, he looked at the sergeant for answers. "She demanded we escort her out here. Said you might shoot her if she just showed up."

"Not if she'd shown up at the sheriff's office. This is my home," Gabriel reminded them, and it wasn't a friendly reminder, either. Her brother obviously didn't want Julia anywhere near the ranch.

"We went there first," the detective answered. "When neither you nor Deputy Doran were there, Ms. Lange wanted us to bring her here so she could give you something. She's not armed—we checked—and she wouldn't give the info to us."

"Because I don't want this to fall into the wrong hands."

Lauren had no idea what Julia had, or rather what

the woman claimed to have, but she shook her head. "You couldn't force her to turn it over to you?"

The sergeant grunted as if he wished he could have done that. "Ms. Lange's not under arrest." He shot Julia a hard glance. "That was before we knew about the loan shark, though. I'll be looking into that."

Good. Lauren hoped SAPD dug until they got to the truth.

"Anyway," the sergeant went on, "your brother-in-law, Theo Canton, and I are old friends, and I thought I'd bring her here as a favor to him. I know he's worried about what's going on with the trouble you had here, and he'd like to put a stop to it. I figured if Ms. Lange could help in any way, that it'd be worth the drive."

Maybe it would be. If not, Lauren was certain that Cameron and Gabriel would put a quick end to this little visit.

Julia gave Cameron a piece of paper that she took from her purse. Lauren looked at it from over his shoulder, but it appeared to be some sort of code.

"That's the password for the computer files," Julia explained. "Files for Alden's business."

Lauren had a closer look, but she didn't recognize the site for the online storage, the password or the files. "I manage my late husband's company," Lauren said to the cops. "These aren't my files, and—"

"No, they're Duane's," Julia interrupted. "He's been keeping secret books from you. No good reason I can think of for doing that, but if you go through those files, you can see there's money missing. Enough to pay some thugs to kill you so he can get the company he believes he should have had all along."

Lauren felt her breath go thin. Of course she'd known Duane could be behind this, but it put an icy chill through her to hear it spelled out like that.

"How did you get this?" Cameron asked her.

Julia pulled back her shoulders. "I was looking for any kind of files or notes my brother might have left before he died."

Translation—Julia wanted to find something she could use for her lawsuit to get Alden's money.

"You hacked into Duane's files," Lauren concluded.

"Company files," Julia corrected. She pointed to the paper. "And I got you something that'll not only clear my name, but you can also use to arrest Duane."

The sergeant turned to Gabriel. "Since the company is in Dallas and the computer hacking happened there, that's out of our jurisdiction. You want to call in your brother Jameson to handle this?"

Since Jameson was a Texas Ranger, he didn't have a set jurisdiction. He could basically do whatever local law enforcement asked him to do.

Gabriel nodded. "I'll have Jameson check it out. If he finds anything, he'll let you know. And if there's nothing else, I'd like for you to get Ms. Lange off Beckett land."

The cops made sounds of agreement. The detective started back to the cruiser with Julia, but Sergeant Welker stayed behind. However, he didn't look at Gabriel but rather Cameron.

"I made some calls on the way over here," the sergeant said. "Just so I could figure out what the devil was going on with Ms. Lange. Anyway, I discovered Evelyn Waters was out of jail. I remembered all the trouble you had with her a few months back."

"Yeah," Cameron verified, "she's out on probation."

"I heard." The sergeant huffed. "I thought you might want to know that she got out early thanks to Judge Wendell Olsen. They're old friends—belong to the same country club and such. Anyway, the only reason I'm bringing it up is because Evelyn's looking to have her record expunged. Then it'll be as if she never even committed the crime."

"Can she do that?" Lauren immediately asked.

"Not without friends in high places," the sergeant answered. "This might not amount to anything, but I heard that Evelyn plans to have Judge Olsen help her get custody of her grandson. Just thought you'd want to know," he added before he walked away.

The chill inside her got even colder. So cold that it caused Lauren to shudder. "I won't let that woman have Patrick or Isaac."

"No," Cameron quietly agreed.

Gabriel shut the door, reactivated the security system and went to the window to watch—making certain that Julia did indeed leave. Lauren headed straight to the nursery, and even though she was moving pretty fast, Cameron caught up with her.

"It's time for us to hide the boys," she insisted. Yes, she was panicking, and she couldn't make herself stop.

Cameron took hold of her arm and stepped in front of her. "Not yet. But there is something we need to do."

"What? Because I'll do anything to keep them safe."

"So will I." Cameron looked her straight in the eyes when he continued. "And that's why you and I need to get married."

Chapter Nine

Cameron hadn't been sure what Lauren's reaction would be when he proposed to her. Or rather when he had *insisted* they get married. He had figured she would be shocked.

And she was.

He had also expected her to need some time to think about it.

And she had.

But what he hadn't counted on was that her thinking time would last through the night. She hadn't even brought it up when Patrick had awakened around two in the morning, and Cameron and she had ended up in the nursery together. Lauren had rocked the baby back to sleep while she hummed to him. What she hadn't done was given Cameron an answer. Or for that matter, she hadn't even talked that much to him. Granted it was an ungodly hour, but still he'd expected something—including a flat-out no answer.

Now it was causing his own round of thinking

time as he sat in the family room with his third cup of coffee and went through the latest emails about the investigation. Cameron had been certain that Lauren would jump on the idea since it might be necessary to stop Evelyn's claim to custody. Even a dirty judge would have trouble explaining why he would deny custody to a married couple and then hand the baby over to a grandmother with a criminal record.

Of course, nothing they did might be enough to stop Evelyn, who seemed hell-bent on raising her grandson. Since she'd done such a bad job raising Trace, Cameron didn't want the woman to have a second chance to screw up another child's life. Especially when that child was Gilly's son.

He downloaded the next round of emails, scowling at the one that caught his eye. It was from Sergeant Welker, SAPD. It was an account by an informant that Welker identified only as a "credible source," who basically repeated what Welker had already told them. Evelyn was gearing up for a fight. Maybe that wouldn't include another attack, but just in case Evelyn did have that on her agenda, Cameron had added even more to their security measures.

Gabriel and he had posted hands on the old trails that coiled around the ranch. It wasn't foolproof since gunmen could still go through the woods to get to them, but there was no way they could watch every acre of land. Cameron could only hope that if thugs did get near the house, then the other hands and reserve deputies would see them and stop them.

The next email didn't cause Cameron's scowl to fade. It was from Jameson, who was now handling the so-called evidence Julia had given them. The Rangers' computer guys had gotten into the files without a hitch, and it did indeed appear that Duane was keeping a second set of books, but it could be something that Julia had set up to incriminate the man. It was going to take time to unravel everything, and time wasn't something that was on their side.

Cameron had a bad feeling in the pit of his stomach.

The feeling eased up a lot, though, when he heard the chatter. Baby talk. He'd seen both boys when they'd gotten up about an hour earlier, but Lauren, Jodi and the nannies had whisked them away for baths and breakfast. That was probably like therapy for them and a good way to get their minds off the danger that seemed to be skulking right up to their doorsteps. That potential danger was the reason Gabriel was working in his home office. Jameson would be returning soon, too, after he finished up some things in Dallas.

The chatter got louder, and Cameron expected to see all the women, including Lauren, come into the room. But it was only Lauren. She had a baby on each hip, and she was smiling. *Really* smiling.

Her happiness faded some, though, when her attention landed on his face. Probably because of his somber expression after reading those emails. Cameron quickly tried to fix that, though. He put his laptop and coffee aside and got to his feet.

"Nothing new on the investigation," Cameron told her right off, and he went to them.

They were a welcome sight, that was for sure. Both boys had obviously had their baths and been fed because they looked ready to do some serious playing. They were squirming to get down—probably because there were some plastic toy blocks on the coffee table.

However, the squirming shifted to a different direction when Isaac reached out for Cameron. He took the boy, brushing a kiss on the top of his head, but Patrick must have wanted a part of that because he reached for Cameron, too. Cameron quickly found his arms filled with babies. Patrick gave him a sloppy kiss on the cheek while Isaac bopped Cameron on the nose.

Lauren laughed.

It was silky and soft, but it faded, though, just as the smile had done.

Lauren picked up two of the blocks and handed both of the boys one. Of course they went straight in their mouths, but it would keep them occupied for a couple of seconds while he chatted with Lauren.

"In case you missed it last night, I did bring up the subject of marriage," Cameron reminded her.

She nodded, then dodged his gaze. On a heavy sigh, Lauren dropped down into the chair next to the sofa. "When I was a teenager, I used to plan our wedding," she said. "You knew that, of course."

He did. He'd heard her talking to Ivy about it. It'd scared the heck out of him, too, because Lauren had been just seventeen. If her father had caught wind of it, he probably would have fired Cameron, punched him or both. Back then, marriage hadn't even been on his radar, but he had been attracted to Lauren. Wisely, he'd held back on the attraction, though, until she had turned eighteen. They'd had just a couple of short weeks together before the night that changed everything.

"Old water, old bridge," she added in a mumble.

Cameron wished that hadn't felt like a slap. Or a lie. It might be old baggage, but the attraction was still just as strong and new as it had been when she'd discussed marrying him with her sister.

As he'd predicted, the boys started to squirm, and he stood them on the floor next to the coffee table so they could reach the rest of the blocks.

"I just thought it would be easier to fight Evelyn if we had a united front," Cameron told her.

Lauren didn't argue with that. In fact, she didn't say anything for several long moments. "I agree. We should get married."

Cameron snapped toward Lauren and stared at her. She didn't look convinced this was the right thing to do, but then, Cameron wasn't so sure it would work, either. Right now they didn't have a lot of ammunition to fight custody with anyone. Not with the DNA results not in yet, and he wasn't going to allow either boy to be placed into foster care.

"I talked this over with Gabriel," Lauren added.

Cameron hadn't figured anything else she could say would surprise him, but that sure did. "And?"

Lauren lifted her shoulder, and without missing a beat, she caught Isaac when he wobbled and nearly fell. She steadied the baby before she looked at Cameron. "He understands."

Yeah, but that was a whole different thing than approving of it. He was reasonably sure that Gabriel no longer held any resentment for Cameron's screwup ten years ago, but he would still want to protect his sister. Lauren's husband had only been dead a year and a half, and Gabriel probably thought it was too soon for her to get married.

And it might be.

But their options were limited here.

"Anyway, I can get started," she went on. She stood, rubbing her hands along the sides of her jeans. "I mean, I can call the courthouse and see about putting a rush on a license."

"I've already done that. Just in case you said yes. I know the clerks who work there, and one of them can bring it over this morning. The justice of the peace can come out, as well, and marry us."

She dragged in a long breath, nodded again. "You've been busy."

"I wanted to save time. My guess is that Evelyn will be visiting her judge friend today if she hasn't already."

Cameron hadn't expected this to be a romantic moment. After all, they were devising a plan to save the children they both loved, but Lauren looked as if she was bracing herself for a huge disaster. Not exactly a way to stroke his ego. Especially after that hot kiss that'd happened just yesterday.

Lauren finally looked him straight in the eyes. "If this marriage arrangement goes south," she said, "please promise me that you won't try to keep either of the boys from me."

"Of course. You'll make the same promise to me?"

"Yes." She stood and fluttered her fingers to the back of the house. "I'll tell the others. Any idea how soon you can get the clerk and justice of the peace out here?"

He took out his phone. "ASAP."

"Good." She took another of those long breaths and repeated it before she scooped up the babies.

Cameron was about to tell her to leave them while she did whatever it was she needed to do, but his phone rang before he could do that. When he saw the name on the screen, he decided it was a call he should take.

Duane.

He showed her the screen, and Lauren put the boys back on the floor. No doubt so she could listen.

"Duane knows the accusations Julia made against him?" she asked.

"He knows. Jameson called him last night." Which meant this probably wasn't going to be a pleasant conversation. Still, Cameron wanted to know what the man had to say about those files.

He didn't put the call on speaker in case Duane started cursing. Even though the boys were too young to understand it, Cameron still didn't want them hearing it. However, he held out the phone between Lauren and him so that she could lean in and listen. She moved to the sofa next to him.

"Why did you have the Texas Rangers come after me?" Duane said without a greeting. Unlike his other conversation with Cameron and Julia, this one did not have a respectful tone to it. "You know anything Julia said about me would be a lie."

"She had computer files," Cameron reminded the man.

"Files that she concocted to make me look guilty." And yes, Duane peppered that with some profanity. "If she gets me out of the way, she has an easier path to getting her brother's company. I can't believe she convinced you that what she found was real."

"She didn't convince us," Lauren said. "But it had to be investigated. That's why Jameson was called in. If the files are bogus, then he'll figure that out."

Duane made a sharp sound of disagreement. "Innocent people get railroaded all the time. In fact, there are plenty who believe Travis Canton was wrongfully convicted of murdering your parents."

That caused the skin to crawl on the back of Cameron's neck, and Lauren didn't seem to fare much better. She clamped her teeth over her bottom lip for a moment, as if trying to keep her composure. Despite the sudden bad turn of mood in the air, the boys thankfully didn't seem to pick up on it. They continued to play with the blocks, banging them against the hardwood floor.

"Why would you bring up Travis?" Cameron demanded from Duane.

"Because it's true. Travis never confessed. Heck, he doesn't even remember if he's guilty. You didn't lock him up that night when you found him drunk, and that made him an easy patsy for someone who needed a scapegoat."

All of that had been in the newspapers, so it wasn't surprising that Duane would know those details. What Cameron wanted to know was why this man was even interested in the old murders.

"How long ago did you file the lawsuit against Lauren and Patrick?" Cameron asked.

Duane hesitated, maybe because he realized he'd just spilled something he shouldn't. "Are you accusing me of something?"

"Just asking a very simple question."

Of course, it wasn't that simple. Cameron wanted to know if the lawsuit was somehow tied to the threatening letters they'd been receiving. Lauren, included. Maybe Duane was trying to intimidate her or send her running by making her believe her parents' "real" killer was going to come after Patrick and her.

"About six months ago," Duane finally answered. Definitely not a trace of friendliness in his voice. "Why?"

"Because shortly after that, Lauren started getting death threats. Did you have something to do with that?"

"No!" No hesitation that time. "Hell, I called you to try to clear up the lies Julia told, and now you accuse me of this?"

"I'm not accusing. Again, I'm just asking a simple question."

"No," Duane repeated, though it sounded as if he'd spoken through clenched teeth. "I didn't threaten Lauren. And I didn't do any creative bookkeeping so I could steal money from the company. I sure as hell didn't hire any gunmen to go after Lauren."

Well, Cameron had gotten his answers, but he wasn't sure if they were the truth or not. There was no way Duane would just confess his wrongdoing, since it could land him in jail. Especially if Jameson could connect any missing funds to the bank accounts of those hired thugs who'd been killed at the ranch. That would be a charge of conspiracy to commit murder and would give Duane plenty of time behind bars.

"Why did you really call?" Cameron pressed.

He expected Duane to shout out his innocence

again. He didn't. "Evelyn Waters called me first thing this morning."

Judging from the way Lauren's eyes widened, that surprised her as much as it did Cameron. "What did she want?"

"To invest in my legal fund to fight Lauren. In exchange, she'll want a piece of the company once I reclaim it."

Hell. Evelyn was really on the offensive, and Cameron thought he knew why she'd gone about it at this angle. Maybe Evelyn thought she could cause Lauren to go broke with a long legal battle. Or maybe just wear Lauren down. It wasn't going to work. Cameron didn't come from money, but Lauren did. And the Becketts would join forces to make sure she had whatever funds she needed. Plus, she could always tap into her trust fund.

"A word of advice about Evelyn," Cameron warned the man. "She could be looking to use you as a patsy. If she breaks the law again, and it sounds as if she's very close to doing that, then she'll want someone to take the fall for her. She could have you in her sights for that."

"I'm not worried about Evelyn," Duane insisted the moment Cameron had finished. "Julia's the snake in all of this. You'd better hope she doesn't team up with Evelyn. With Evelyn's seemingly unlimited supply of cash and Julia's desperation, it could be an unholy alliance."

Yeah, one that could have already happened. Evelyn could have given Julia the cash to pay those gunmen. That way, if Evelyn managed to kill both Lauren and him, she'd have a better shot at getting her hands on the baby.

"If Julia's the snake you think she is," Lauren said, "then we need proof to stop her. Do you have anything we can use? Something more than just her owing money to a loan shark."

"That should be enough," Duane snapped. But then he huffed. "I'll look and see what I can find. I have some incentive now that Julia's set the dogs on me with those fake files."

Cameron jumped right on that. "If they're truly fake, then figure out a way to prove that. The Rangers are looking into it, of course, but they could use your help."

He wasn't so sure of that. In fact, Jameson might not want any interference from a suspect, but it could keep Duane busy. Of course, if Duane was behind the attacks, then this was all just a ruse anyway. The man could have called them just to keep the focus on those files rather than the fact that someone was trying to kill them.

"Find something to put Julia behind bars," Cameron repeated to Duane, and he ended the call.

During the conversation, Cameron had glanced at Lauren a few times while also keeping an eye on the boys, but he really looked at her now. There were no tears in her eyes, but he saw that this was taking a serious toll on her. It was the same for him, too.

"Marrying you might not help," she said, her voice a whisper.

"It might not." Cameron had thought about all angles of this, and there was one angle that he needed to mention. "If we're married and one of us dies, then the other one would have a legal claim to the boys. We'd need to do guardianship paperwork, of course. And wills."

Hell, that caused Lauren to go way too pale, and he reached for her, pulling her into his arms. The embrace didn't last, though. Isaac lost his balance again, and Lauren bolted from the sofa. This time she didn't get to him in time, and the baby fell. He didn't hit hard, but it was enough to cause him to start crying. The commotion must have upset Patrick because he started to cry, as well.

Lauren scooped up both boys, kissing them, and Cameron went to her to help. He didn't get far, though, because his phone rang again. The sound of it only caused the babies to cry even louder. Lauren motioned for him to take the call while she took the babies in the direction of the kitchen.

Cameron figured this might be Duane calling back, but it wasn't a name or number he recognized. He pushed the answer button and hoped it wasn't someone from the press wanting a story. There'd already been a couple of those calls, and he didn't want another. Especially since he had "wedding" arrangements to make.

"Deputy Doran," he answered.

But the caller didn't say anything, and it put a knot in his stomach. Was this another hired gun?

"What do you want?" Cameron snapped.

"Uh, I'm Maria Black," the caller finally said.

He mentally repeated the name, and it rang a bell, but Cameron couldn't make the connection of why it seemed familiar.

"I was a nurse at the hospital where your sister, Gilly Doran, had her son," the woman added several moments later.

Bingo. Now he remembered. He'd spoken to her briefly after learning Gilly was dead. Other than her name, Cameron couldn't recall anything else about her. But just the fact that she had gotten in touch with him piqued his interest.

"Is something wrong?" he asked. Because it was possible that Evelyn was harassing her in some way.

"Yes." Her voice cracked, and it sounded as if she was crying. "I think someone's trying to kill me."

That was not what Cameron wanted to hear. "You need to go to the cops now. Where are you?"

"I'm on my way to the Blue River Sheriff's Office right now, and I need to see you. Lauren, too. God, I'm so sorry, Deputy Doran."

The knot in his stomach got worse. "Sorry for what?"

The sound of her sob was loud and clear. "I wouldn't have done it, but your sister begged me to help her. She was dying, and she begged me to do it. Please forgive me. I'm the one who switched the babies."

Chapter Ten

Lauren sat in the back of the cruiser, staring out the window but not really seeing anything. She felt numb. Of course, she'd known in her heart that the boys had been switched, but she hadn't prepared herself to hear the proof of that.

If it was the truth, that is.

She hadn't gotten a chance to speak to the woman who'd called Cameron, but there had indeed been a nurse named Maria Black who had worked at the hospital where Lauren and Gilly had had their sons. And while it wouldn't have been easy, Maria would have been in a position to make the switch. That didn't mean she had, though.

"Evelyn could have put the nurse up to doing this," Lauren said to Cameron and Gabriel. Her brother was behind the wheel of the cruiser, and Cameron was in the backseat with her.

Judging from their quick sound of approval, the two had already come to that conclusion. "Do you remember Gilly ever mentioning this nurse?" Cameron asked.

"No. But she was on the ward where we were. And Gilly was desperate to keep her baby from Trace. He was still alive then, and she was terrified of him."

That caused a muscle to flicker in Cameron's jaw. It was obviously a sore subject that his kid sister had been in an abusive relationship. One that he hadn't been able to stop. But then, Gilly had kept a lot from him because she'd been worried that Cameron might kill Trace if he learned that Trace made a habit of beating her up.

"When we get to the sheriff's office, I'll ask Maria to take a polygraph," Gabriel said. "It's not conclusive, but if she's lying, it might spur her into telling the truth." He paused. "You do know I'll have to arrest her, right?"

Lauren nodded. She was torn between hating the woman and wanting to thank her for trying to keep Gilly's child safe. Of course, by doing that, Maria had put their lives in a tailspin.

"I can't think of a reason why Julia or Duane would do a baby switch," Lauren tossed out there.

"They could have hoped to prove Patrick wasn't Alden's child," he reminded her. "That might help Julia's lawsuit to get her brother's estate. It might help Duane's cause, too."

True, but that seemed a stretch. Not for Evelyn, though. She might have thought it would be easier for her to kidnap Patrick since Lauren wouldn't have been on the lookout for the woman. Still, it might not have been anything that complicated. Because Maria could be telling the truth.

"I'm guessing you two will go through with this marriage while you're here?" Gabriel asked.

Lauren hadn't been expecting his question. Though she should have. She knew that Cameron had told Gabriel about their plan to wed. She also knew her brother didn't approve. To him it probably seemed like a knee-jerk reaction, one that Cameron and she might regret later. And they might. But doing something—anything—felt better than just spinning her wheels.

"What the hell?" Gabriel mumbled, and he slowed the cruiser.

Since they were still a good mile from town, that put Lauren's heart in her throat, but it took her a moment to figure out what had caused her brother to say that. There was a car just ahead, parked on the shoulder. The driver's door was wide-open.

"You recognize the car?" she asked.

"No," Gabriel and Cameron answered together.

Definitely not good. This wasn't a heavily traveled section of the farm road. In fact, the only traffic was usually from people who lived nearby, but there was a way to access the road from the interstate so occasionally people would take the wrong exit and then look for a turnaround.

"Get down on the seat," Cameron told her.

Lauren had already felt the surge of adrenaline,

and that caused her to feel even more. Her breathing was already too fast. Her heart was throbbing in her ears. She did start to move lower but not before she got a glimpse of someone slumped behind the wheel of the car.

A woman.

One Lauren thought she recognized.

"I think that's Maria Black," she managed to say before Cameron pushed her down on the seat.

"There's blood," Gabriel grumbled.

That sent her heartbeat up another notch, and Lauren immediately thought the worst. Easy to do since Maria had said someone might be trying to kill her. Mercy, had some hired thugs gotten to her before she could make it into town?

After Gabriel called for an ambulance, he stopped directly next to Maria's car, and Lauren had another look just to make sure it was indeed the woman. It was.

And, yes, there was blood.

It was on the side of her head. Maria's face was turned toward them with her head resting on the steering wheel. Lauren was about to ask if she was dead, but then she saw the woman move.

"Stay in the cruiser with Lauren," Gabriel told Cameron.

Lauren could tell he didn't want to do that. Cameron wanted to be out there helping his boss, but he stayed put. However, he did open the door a fraction and drew his gun.

Because the person who'd injured Maria could still be around.

Keeping low, Lauren glanced around, trying to spot anyone else in the area. There weren't many trees on this stretch of land, only pasture, so it would be hard for someone to hide. But then she remembered one of the goons at the ranch who'd hidden in the ditch outside Cameron's house. There were plenty of ditches, including one that was just to the right of Maria's car.

"Be careful," she warned her brother.

Gabriel also drew his gun and went to Maria. Lauren couldn't hear what he said to her or vice versa, but she did see the woman's lips move. Maria didn't seem strong enough, though, to lift her head, and she didn't open her eyes. Lauren couldn't tell if that was because the woman was dazed or if she was dying. Yes, there was blood, but it didn't seem like there was enough to indicate she was bleeding out. It was possible she'd had to slam on her brakes and hadn't been wearing her seat belt. Her head could have hit the steering wheel. She certainly had seemed frantic when she'd called them, and people in a panic made mistakes.

"Maybe it won't take long for the ambulance to get here," Lauren muttered. And while she was hoping, Lauren added that whatever Maria was saying to Gabriel, that it would help them figure out what the heck was going on.

Gabriel took Maria's hand and had her press it to

her side. Maybe that meant she was injured there, as well, and her brother had done that to make sure the wound didn't bleed too much. After Gabriel had done that, he came by the side of the cruiser.

"She says someone rammed into the rear end of her car," Gabriel explained. He wasn't looking at them, though. Like Cameron, he was keeping watch around them. "A big bulky guy got out of the other vehicle, came up to her and shot her at point-blank range."

Oh, mercy. Lauren had to put her hand to her chest to try to steady her heart. "How is she still alive then?"

"My guess is she won't be for long. The bullet appears to have grazed her head, but she was shot in the chest, too."

Cameron cursed. "What did Maria say to you?"

"She only said one word, and she kept repeating it." Gabriel paused. "Julia."

The air was suddenly so still that it felt as if everything was holding its breath. Everything including Lauren.

"Julia's behind this," Lauren heard herself whisper.

"Or someone wanted Maria to believe she was," Cameron quickly pointed out.

Yes, that was possible. Julia had perhaps tried to set up Duane, and now he could be doing the same to her. But why would he, or Julia for that matter, hire someone to murder Maria?

Gabriel's head whipped up, his attention going in the direction of the road behind him, where she heard the sounds of someone slamming on their brakes. Lauren hoped it was just someone who belonged out here, someone who was stopping to see if they could help.

But judging from Gabriel's expression, he didn't think that.

Neither did Cameron. He pushed Lauren all the way down on the seat, and Gabriel ran back to the cruiser. However, before her brother could get back in, Lauren heard another sound.

Someone fired a shot.

CAMERON DIDN'T HAVE much time to react. In the blink of an eye, the shooter leaned out from the SUV, sent a bullet slamming into the cruiser and ducked back behind the heavily tinted glass. Almost immediately, the driver sped up, and Cameron knew they were about to slam into them.

He didn't have to tell Gabriel to hurry. He was. But Cameron did have to warn Lauren again to keep down. She was obviously terrified for her brother. And she should be. Gabriel was literally out in the open, and another shot could kill him.

However, the gunman didn't fire again. That was because the SUV did plow right into them, jolting them forward.

Cameron's shoulder smacked into the back of the seat, the impact so hard that the pain jackknifed through him. But that was the least of his worries. The impact also caused the cruiser to collide right into Gabriel. Lauren shouted out to him as he fell to the ground.

Now more shots came. Three of them, and Cameron had to fight to regain not only his balance but his aim, too. Hell, he was hurting, but he pushed that aside and threw open the door that had slammed shut during the collision. He had to return fire. Had to keep these thugs from killing Gabriel.

Cameron leaned out of the cruiser, took aim at the SUV's front windshield and started firing. The glass was obviously bulletproof, but his shots were doing some damage. They were causing the glass to crack, and maybe that would be enough to obstruct the driver's view.

It wasn't enough for the gunman, though.

The thug's hand came out from the passenger-side window, and he fired at Cameron. Cameron had to scramble back, and in the same motion, he pushed Lauren onto the floor in case the glass on the cruiser gave way.

"My brother," she said on a rise of breath.

He couldn't see Gabriel, which meant he was probably pinned down in front of the cruiser. He couldn't stay there because Cameron needed him back in so they could get the heck out of there. That meant trying to get Maria into the cruiser, as well.

Cameron took out his backup weapon from the side holster in his jeans and handed it to Lauren.

"This doesn't mean I want you getting up and returning fire," he warned her. "I want you to have it just in case."

What he meant was in case all else failed and those goons made it to her. If that happened, it would mean they would have already shot Gabriel and him.

"What are you going to do?" Her voice was shaking like the rest of her.

Something that wouldn't be particularly safe, but then, nothing was safe right now. He gave her his phone, as well. "Make sure we have some backup on the way out here."

That wasn't just busywork, either. Cameron wasn't sure if Gabriel had requested assistance when he'd called the ambulance, and if he hadn't, Cameron needed more deputies on the way now.

"They're coming," Lauren relayed to him a few seconds later. "But the ambulance can't get in here as long as shots are being fired."

Yeah, he'd known that would be the case, but he had to try.

"Don't get up," he told Lauren one last time.

He threw his door all the way open, using it for cover. Not just for him but for Gabriel, too.

"We need to get Maria," Cameron said to Gabriel.

Cameron didn't shout it because he didn't want to telegraph his moves to the gunmen, but they likely couldn't have heard anyway because the bullets were slamming nonstop into the cruiser. It wasn't only the passenger firing, either. The driver had gotten in on the shooting.

Gabriel came around the side of the cruiser. He didn't appear hurt—thank God—and he opened the front door. Cameron didn't lean out far enough to make himself a target, but he fired some shots at the gunmen, hoping he would get lucky and hit one of them. He didn't, but at least it caused them to pull their hands back into the SUV. That gave Gabriel and him a few precious seconds to rescue Maria.

Even though Gabriel had said the nurse probably wasn't going to make it, Cameron couldn't leave her there to die. The thugs would likely just shoot her again, and this time, they would finish her off.

Cameron and Gabriel both took hold of Maria, dragging her out of her car and into the front of the cruiser. Gabriel climbed over her, getting behind the wheel, and Cameron scrambled to get in the backseat. He almost made it, too.

But the SUV slammed into them again.

Cameron heard Lauren call out to him. He heard Gabriel curse, too, but he couldn't respond. That was because the impact caused the still open back door to smack against his head. His arm and shoulder were still hurting, but this was a whole new level of pain. Worse, it dazed him enough so that it blurred his vision.

The shots started coming at him again, the bullets tearing through the metal in the door. Cameron groped around, trying to orient himself, but he was pretty sure he was failing. Until someone caught on to his arm and pulled him onto the backseat of the cruiser. He landed against the seat and came up, ready to fire.

But Lauren fired first.

That was when he realized one of the thugs was right there. Just a few feet away from him. The guy had obviously gotten out of the SUV with plans to get close enough to kill him. And that was exactly what he would have done if Lauren hadn't put a bullet in his head.

The shooter dropped to the ground.

Seeing his partner fall must have enraged the driver because he slammed the SUV into them again.

"Hold on," Gabriel warned them a split second before he gunned the engine and sped off.

The jolt tossed Cameron and Lauren around again, and it didn't help that the SUV managed to ram them one more time.

Cameron got his door shut, and he pivoted in the seat to try to figure out what he could do. Not much. The front of the SUV had almost certainly been reinforced, but there wasn't much damage to it. That meant the driver had no trouble coming at them again. Gabriel pushed the accelerator even more, trying to get them out of there.

Despite the ringing in his ears, Cameron heard a welcome sound. Sirens. Backup had arrived. But the thug in the SUV no doubt heard them, as well, because he slammed on his brakes. The road wasn't that wide, but he managed to get turned around in just a few seconds.

And he drove off.

Cameron wanted to go after the SOB and beat the truth out of him. He wanted to find out who'd hired him and his dead partner to try to kill them. But it was too risky to do that. Instead, Gabriel instructed the backup to go after the SUV while he continued to drive toward town. It didn't take long for the SUV to disappear from sight.

Lauren's hands were shaking hard, but she was able to use his phone to call the ranch. "The SUV might go there," she said.

That upped his concern a couple of notches. Even though he knew there were plenty of security measures in place, Cameron didn't release the breath he'd been holding until he heard Jameson tell Lauren that all was well at the ranch. The babies were fine.

Two cruisers went flying past them, heading in the same direction as the SUV. Cameron only hoped they could catch up with him and bring the snake in alive for questioning.

Gabriel kept volleying glances in the rearview mirror and at Maria, but he also made a call to the sheriff's office.

"Are you okay?" Cameron asked Lauren.

She nodded. "But you're not. Your head is bleeding."

"I'm fine." That was possibly the truth, and even

if it wasn't, Cameron had no plans to do anything about it.

He cupped Lauren's face, checking for any injuries but didn't see any. However, there was a new level of fear in her eyes. Of course, she had just killed a man. Her second one in two days. It would only add to the other nightmares she already had.

"How about you?" he asked Gabriel. "Are you hurt?"

"Just some bruises." He tipped his head to Maria. "She can't say the same, though."

No. Now that the woman was in the cruiser, Cameron had no trouble seeing that the front of her dress was drenched in blood. Cameron pulled off his shirt and held it to her chest wound. It wasn't much, but maybe it would help until they could get her to the hospital.

"What about the ambulance?" Lauren asked. "How soon can it get here now that the shots have stopped?"

"It's just about a half mile up," Gabriel answered. "I talked to Jace at the office, and he said they're waiting for us."

Good. That would mean Maria would soon get the medical attention she needed.

"Julia," Cameron heard Maria mumble. Her voice was too weak, and he wasn't sure if she could manage more than just that one word, but Cameron had to try.

"Did Julia hire the men who did this to you?" Cameron asked.

Maria opened her eyes, and it was as if she was surprised he was there. "Deputy Doran," she said. Her gaze drifted to Lauren. "I'm so sorry."

"The apology can wait." Cameron hated to sound harsh, but hearing that wasn't going to help them. "Why do you keep saying Julia's name?"

Maria dragged in a shallow breath. "She came to see me."

Probably not a good thing especially since Julia was desperate for money. "You told her about the baby swap?"

Maria nodded, and her eyes drifted down. "Be careful."

It was definitely a warning, but Cameron didn't get a chance to press her for more. That was because Gabriel hit the brakes again. This time, though, it was for the ambulance. He pulled to a quick stop right next to it, and the medics rushed out to take Maria.

"I'll ride with her to the hospital," Cameron insisted.

With the seconds ticking away, he figured he only had a few minutes at most to get what he needed from Maria. The truth. And then maybe he could finally put an end to this once and for all.

Chapter Eleven

Lauren sat at Gabriel's desk and waited. Something she'd been doing since they'd arrived at the sheriff's office over an hour ago. There wasn't much else she could do until Cameron called with news from the hospital.

Maybe the news would be good. Maybe Maria would survive surgery and be able to tell them what was going on. Until then, Cameron had no plans to leave.

At least the boys weren't anywhere near the danger and the aftermath. Lauren hadn't been able to stop herself from calling Dara three times to make sure all was well there. It was. And now she had to pray it stayed that way.

She heard the footsteps heading toward her, and Lauren practically jumped to her feet. But it wasn't Cameron. It was Gabriel. He had a foam box in one hand, a bottle of water in the other, and he was sporting a very concerned look.

"A sandwich from the diner," he said, putting the

box and water on the desk in front of her. "You need to eat."

Yes, she probably did, but she wasn't hungry. In fact, her stomach was churning. Still, she would try to keep something down. It wouldn't do any of them any good if she got light-headed.

"Anything from Cameron?" she asked, but she already knew the answer. If there had been, Cameron would have texted her. He knew she was on pins and needles while she waited.

He shook his head and opened the foam box when she didn't touch it. Lauren sat down and took a small bite of the BLT. There wasn't just one sandwich, though, but two. Gabriel must have thought she was starved. Or just eager to sample something she hadn't had in a long time.

"You remembered this was my favorite," she said. He'd even gotten a bag of her favorite chips to go with it.

"Of course I remembered. You're my sister."

There was some emotion that went with that comment, and Lauren knew they were talking about a lot more than just the sandwich.

She looked up at him, their eyes connecting. "I can't apologize for leaving Blue River. I *had* to go."

If he agreed with that, he didn't show any signs of it. "Now you're back." He paused, a muscle flickering in his jaw. "With plans to marry Cameron."

There was definitely no hint of agreement for that,

either. "We don't want any chance of the boys being sent to foster care."

Gabriel nodded. Finally, they'd found some common ground. "And then what? What do you do when we stop the person behind the attacks?"

At least he'd said *when* and not *if.* This had to stop. They couldn't keep going on like this.

"I don't know," she answered honestly. "When the DNA tests prove there's been a swap—"

"There was," Gabriel interrupted. "I just got the results back. I texted Cameron, too, so he knows."

Obviously, Lauren had known the swap had taken place, but it still felt like a shock. A violation, really. Someone—Maria, probably—had swapped the babies, and in doing so had robbed Lauren of being with her son for the first year of his life. She'd done the same to Cameron.

"I love Patrick just as much as I do Isaac," she said, pushing the sandwich aside. No way could she take another bite.

"I know. Cameron feels the same way."

He did. Lauren had no doubts about that, either. "That's another reason for the marriage. Neither of us can give up the babies we've been raising."

Gabriel stayed quiet for a moment. "So you…what? Try to make a real go of it?" He didn't wait for an answer. "Because if you're not, then that's not right for Cameron or you. Especially Cameron. You've had a marriage, a real one, but Cameron's never had that. He deserves it."

Lauren was already reeling from the DNA news and everything else that'd happened, but that only added to the feeling. She hadn't expected her brother to have that objection.

But he was right.

Cameron did deserve better. He deserved a real wife who loved him and wanted to build a family with him. Lauren could give him the family—that was already in place—but she wasn't sure she could handle the rest. A real marriage to Cameron would mean her staying in Blue River. It would mean forgetting her past. And she wasn't sure she could do that just yet.

"What are you suggesting?" she came out and asked.

"That you hold off on saying I do at least for a day or so until you've had time to give it more thought."

Good advice. But it wasn't advice she could take. "It would crush me if the boys were taken away. In fact, I couldn't let that happen, and that means Cameron and I could end up breaking the law."

Gabriel gave her a snarled look that only a lawman big brother could manage, and he made a suit-yourself sound. Since she'd obviously ruffled his feathers, Lauren went to him and brushed a kiss on his cheek. She hadn't expected it to help and was surprised when it did. It soothed his expression a bit anyway.

"I love you," he said. "I only want the best for you. For Jameson, Cameron and Ivy, too."

She knew that. So did they. But there were no easy ways for her to get "the best." Right now she'd just settle for keeping the babies and the rest of them safe.

"I love you, too," Lauren answered.

They had a nice moment, one that felt like old times before Gabriel tipped his head to the sandwich. "You should finish eating. You're going to need your strength. Duane and Julia are on their way here now."

That wouldn't be fun, but it was necessary. "They agreed to come?"

Gabriel gave her a flat look. "I didn't exactly ask. I told them I'd put out warrants for their arrests if they didn't show up. I want to question Julia especially."

Yes, because Maria had kept repeating the woman's name.

"I thought if I had Julia and Duane here together, that one of them might blurt out something when they started arguing with each other," Gabriel went on. "There seems to be enough bad blood between them that it brings out the fangs."

It did. And the two had had no trouble incriminating each other in their other conversations. Too bad nothing had panned out on those so Gabriel could make an arrest. There'd been no proof that Julia had hired those gunmen, and the Rangers hadn't had any luck confirming that the files Julia gave them were real and not some attempt to set up Duane.

"And Evelyn?" she asked. "Are you bringing her in, too?"

Gabriel got that hard look again. "She's not an-

swering her phone, and according to her housekeeper, she didn't come home last night."

Lauren thought about that for a moment. "Could
she be with her *friend*, Judge Olsen?"

Gabriel shook his head. "I called him. He didn't
know where she was, either. I pressed him for some
info about his relationship with Evelyn." He put relationship in air quotes. "But he got huffy and reminded me that I was a small-town cop who had no
right to question him."

"That sounds like something a guilty man would
say. Please tell me there's something that proves
Evelyn has bought off Judge Olsen?"

"Nothing. So far," he quickly added. "I'm hoping either Julia or Duane will have something to
say about that, too. All three—Duane, Julia and
Evelyn—seemed to be coiled around each other like
a family of snakes."

They did. And that was unsettling. It was bad
enough if only one of them was behind this, but if
they'd teamed up…well, Lauren didn't want to go
there.

She heard more footsteps, and Lauren hurried to
get past Gabriel so she could peer out into the hall.
Gabriel didn't let her get far, though. He stepped in
front of her, probably because he thought it was one
of their suspects. It wasn't.

It was Cameron.

He was wearing a bandage on the side of his head
near his right temple, but even seeing that didn't di-

minish the relief she felt. It flooded through her, and Lauren practically ran to him. She hadn't intended to do it, but she put her arms around him and kissed him.

Cameron's muscles tensed, probably because he hadn't been expecting it. And because Gabriel was almost certainly watching them. Still, Cameron didn't push her away. He let the kiss linger until Lauren eased back.

And that was when she saw the weariness in his eyes. Lauren was pretty sure she knew what it meant, too.

"Maria's dead?" she asked.

He nodded and brushed a kiss on her cheek. Not a kiss of relief as hers had been. Also not one of passion. That had been meant to comfort her, and much to her surprise, it worked.

She'd been right about Gabriel watching them. He was in the doorway, but he walked out, stopping directly in front of them. "Did Maria say anything else?"

"No." Cameron scrubbed his hand over his face and blew out a long, frustrated breath. "She was unconscious by the time she went into surgery, and she died on the operating table."

Lauren reminded herself that the woman's chances of surviving hadn't been that good, but it was still a blow. Not just because they wouldn't be able to get answers from her but also because a woman was dead. Maria hadn't exactly been innocent since she was the one who'd switched the babies, but she didn't deserve to die because of what she'd done.

"Whoever's behind this can now be charged with murder," Gabriel said.

He was right, but the trick would be to catch the person.

As if waiting for something, Gabriel glanced at both Cameron and her. Maybe he wanted to discuss the marriage, but he didn't get a chance to do that. That was because his phone rang. When he glanced at the screen, he mumbled something about having to take the call, and he went into the squad room.

"Make sure she eats," Gabriel told Cameron from over his shoulder. "Her lunch is on my desk."

Cameron immediately took her back into her brother's office, and she was about to remind him that he needed to eat, too, but he sat across from her and helped himself to some of the chips. She handed him half the sandwich, and he started in on that, as well.

"You know about Duane, Julia and Evelyn?" she asked.

He nodded, then drank some of her water, too. It seemed...intimate or something. Which her body thought was good. Of course, her body often had thoughts like that around Cameron.

"SAPD is looking for Evelyn," he explained, which meant Cameron had been keeping up with the case even when he'd been at the hospital. "The justice of the peace will be here soon, too."

He took something from his shirt pocket and handed it to her. A marriage license.

"I had the clerk bring it to the hospital," Cameron added. He ate more of the chips and stared at her. "Having second thoughts? Or did Gabriel talk you out of doing this?"

"He tried," she admitted. And paused. "FYI. You deserve better, though. Better than a marriage of convenience."

The corner of his mouth kicked up in a slight smile, and he leaned across the desk to drop a kiss on her cheek. "Lauren, there's nothing convenient about you," he drawled

There it was. The heat that always went to flames. It set off red flags in her head. Because the heat could lead her to do things that shouldn't be happening. At least not now anyway. Cameron and she had too much without adding sex to the mix.

The heat faded considerably when she heard the voices in the squad room. Julia and Duane had arrived. And they'd brought their lawyers from the sound of it. Someone—a man—was talking about this being harassment.

"I haven't started to harass you yet," Gabriel growled, his voice low and dangerous as only Gabriel could manage. "Trust me, you'll know when I've started."

Cameron and she stepped into the hall just as she saw Gabriel motioning for Duane and Julia to follow him. Lauren had been right about the lawyers.

There was a man and woman, both wearing business clothes, and they fell in step behind Gabriel as he led them toward the interview room.

Julia stopped to give Lauren a glare.

Lauren glared back and hoped she wouldn't lose her temper and punch the woman. Julia had been a thorn in her side for years, and Lauren had reached her limit. So that her brother wouldn't have to arrest her for assault, she stayed just slightly behind Cameron when they went into the interview room with the others.

"They're going to stay for this?" the female lawyer balked.

"Yes," Gabriel said without hesitation. "And rein in your attitude. Just a short while ago, the three of us had thugs shoot a lot of bullets at us. They killed a woman. And before that woman died, she said one thing—the name of your client. I think Cameron, Lauren and I deserve a few answers about that."

"What?" Julia had just sat down, but that brought her right back to her feet. "That nurse said I did this?"

Obviously, Julia knew plenty about this situation, and judging from her lawyer's scowl, she didn't like that her client had just admitted as much.

Gabriel put his hands on the metal table and leaned in, his face getting very close to Julia's. "Tell me everything you know about *that nurse*."

Duane huffed. "I don't know why I got called in for this. Obviously, this is Julia up to her old tricks again." He got up to leave, too, but Cameron shot him a glare that could have frozen Texas in August.

"Sit," Cameron said through clenched teeth.

Duane sat, but his lawyer—the bald guy in a gray suit—rattled off a legal protest. He didn't mention the word *harassment*, though.

"Your client has the means, motive and opportunity to be behind that attack," Gabriel reminded the lawyer. "That's why he's here. And that's why he's staying here until I get answers. Don't," he added when the lawyer opened his mouth. "I have enough to arrest your client, and I'm in a bad enough mood to do it. Just let Deputy Doran and me ask the questions, and we might be able to get to the bottom of this."

Maybe it was the badass looks on Cameron's and her brother's faces, but the lawyers, Duane and Julia didn't say anything.

Gabriel waited a couple of seconds, and he turned back to Julia. *"That nurse,"* he repeated. "Start talking."

Julia didn't do that right away. She took a deep breath first. "I went to see her. You already knew I was suspicious about Patrick. Because he doesn't look like Alden or me. Or Lauren, for that matter. I'd hoped Lauren had cheated on my brother, that the baby was someone else's. Like *his*." She motioned toward Cameron. "It's obvious Lauren still has feelings for him."

It probably was obvious. Lauren sighed. This old attraction was hard to hide.

"Anyway, Maria didn't admit it at first," Julia went on, "but she finally said she'd switched the babies. She claims she did that because of his sister, Gilly." She pointed to Cameron again. "Gilly was afraid of her baby's father, Trace Waters. Well, I thought that was a stupid reason to do the switch because Trace could have gone after the wrong kid. He could have gone after my nephew."

Julia probably wanted them to think that she cared if that happened or not. She didn't. It would make Julia's lawsuit a little easier if Alden's son wasn't around to be his rightful heir.

"Did Maria happen to say how she did the switch?" Cameron asked.

"I didn't ask about that, but Maria claimed she never intended to put my nephew in danger. She said Gilly had told Trace that the baby wasn't his, and that she would prove it with a DNA test. She had Maria do a test on Alden's son and was having the results sent to Trace. That way, he wouldn't try to take the baby."

That helped soothe Lauren's nerves a bit. At least Gilly had had a plan to protect Isaac. And if Trace had insisted on repeating the DNA test, he would have assumed Gilly had been telling the truth about the boy not being his. Still, there was something not right about this.

"Why didn't Maria tell us what she'd done after Gilly's boyfriend was killed?" Lauren pressed.

"How should I know?" Julia snarled. "I only saw the woman once."

"Yet she kept repeating your name when she was dying." Gabriel stared at her, clearly waiting for an explanation about that.

But an explanation didn't come from Julia. It came from Duane.

"Julia met with Maria more than once," Duane said. Julia opened her mouth as if to shout out a denial, but Duane added, "I have proof."

"You can't possibly have proof—" But Julia stopped, her eyes narrowing. "You had me followed."

"I did," Duane readily admitted. "I wish I'd had you watched 24/7 because that way you wouldn't have had the chance to set up those fake books to try to get me in hot water."

"You had no right," Julia spat out as if she was completely innocent in all of this, and she looked ready to launch herself at Duane.

Cameron got in between them. He pointed to Julia. "How about telling us the truth? Not just about Maria but everything else."

"I have told the truth," she insisted. She paused. "Other than the number of times I met with Maria. What does it matter if I met with her once or three times? It doesn't," she quickly concluded.

Cameron huffed. "It matters because you lied. Now, I want to know why."

Julia made a sound of outrage, and she pushed away her lawyer when she tried to whisper something to Julia.

"I didn't see the point in Maria telling Lauren and you what happened," Julia finally explained. "I mean, you were both raising the babies, and it would only send things into a tailspin."

It didn't take long for Lauren to figure out what Julia had done. And what she'd intended to do. "You paid Maria hush money. Or you could have silenced her by threatening to turn her in to the cops. Of course, you didn't plan to keep it a secret. My guess is you were going to spring the DNA results during the lawsuit. That way, it would negate Patrick's claim to Alden's money."

"Bingo," Duane agreed. "And the reason Julia didn't spill the news sooner was because she didn't want to give you time to figure out what was going on. She was counting on you being stunned enough to just hand over the money to her."

"And it might have worked," Lauren said over the profanity Julia was aiming at Duane. "Except I also got suspicious and had a DNA test done. I would have known the results and had time to figure out what they meant long before the lawsuit."

"That's why Julia hired the gunmen." Duane, again.

Julia went after Duane, this time slamming into Cameron. Her lawyer caught on to her, and between Cameron and her, they managed to get Julia back in her seat.

"My client shouldn't have to sit here and listen to these allegations," the lawyer snapped.

"They're not allegations," Duane responded without hesitating. "Julia came to me months ago and wanted us to team up against Lauren. She thought there was something I could do to drive Lauren back into Cameron's bed. That way, Lauren might decide the lawsuits weren't worth fighting. I mean, it's not like Lauren needs the money or anything."

Gabriel glanced at Lauren, and even though he didn't come out and say it, this was probably what he'd had in mind when he wanted them all in the room together. Obviously, Duane and Julia had been trying to figure out how to get their hands on Alden's money and company.

Julia was glaring. Not just at Duane, either. She shared that glare with Cameron and Lauren. "You have no proof I've done something wrong."

"But we do," Cameron assured her. "You met with a criminal suspect—Maria. You knew she'd committed a crime, and you didn't tell the cops. That definitely falls into the 'done something wrong' category."

Julia sputtered out some angry sounds and slid back her chair, scraping the metal legs against the floor. She got to her feet. "Duane doctored the company books, and I don't see you harassing him like you're doing to me."

"Oh, I'll get to him," Gabriel said. His phone dinged with a text message, and he glanced at the screen before returning his attention to Julia. "Duane knew about Maria's crime, too, and didn't report it. That means both of you are going to stay for a while as my deputies take your statements. I'll have a little chat with the DA to see if he wants me to go ahead and arrest you."

That started more protests from Julia, Duane and their attorneys. They were all so loud that it was nearly impossible to hear what any of them were saying. Gabriel ignored them all and turned to Cameron and her.

"Wait here," Gabriel added to Julia and Duane, and he motioned for Cameron and Lauren to follow him into the hall. Her brother didn't say anything, though, until he'd shut the interview room door. "Maybe they won't kill each other before I get Jace in there to take their statements." He tipped his head to the squad room. "By the way, you two have a visitor."

So that was what the text had been about. And Lauren soon saw who the visitor was. Henry McCoy. He'd been the justice of the peace for as long as Lauren could remember.

Cameron looked at her. The kind of look that implied he was trying to figure out what she was thinking. Was she still up for this? Or was she having second thoughts?

The answer to both questions was yes. Lauren wasn't sure this was the right thing to do, but she was going through with it. She gave Cameron a nod. Her brother must have known what that meant because he huffed. However, Gabriel didn't try to talk her out of it. He walked on ahead of them, making his way to Jace's desk. No doubt to tell the deputy to get started with those statements.

"Thank you for coming," Cameron told Henry. He went to the man and shook his hand.

"Cameron, Lauren," Henry greeted. The man was in his early seventies now, and he seemed frail in a suit that practically hung off him. His smile seemed genuine, though. "Always figured you two would tie the knot." His smile faded. "I hate that it's under these circumstances, though."

It didn't surprise Lauren that Henry knew about the attacks. Or that Cameron and she had once had a thing for each other. Heck, he might even know about the baby swap.

Henry looked around. "You want to say the vows out here or in one of the offices? Oh, and you don't need a witness, but maybe you'd like Gabriel to be there."

Lauren wasn't so sure Gabriel would want to do that, but she turned to ask him. Before she could do that, though, Cameron's phone rang, and she saw Jodi's name on the screen. It gave her another jolt of adrenaline, and it must have done the same to Cameron because he quickly answered it and put the call on speaker.

"Cam, you need to get back to the ranch ASAP. There's been some trouble." Jodi paused. "Evelyn's here."

Chapter Twelve

Cameron hated that he was having to rush Lauren out of the sheriff's office. When they were in a panic, it was hard to think straight, and with a mind-set like that, it could make them easy targets for those hired guns who were still out there. Still, Cameron didn't have a choice.

He couldn't let Evelyn get anywhere near the babies.

"Where's Evelyn now?" Cameron asked Jodi.

"I'm holding her at gunpoint. I had Jameson stay inside with the boys."

Good. Even though Gabriel had plenty of work to do, he must have heard what Jodi said because he grabbed the keys for the cruiser that was parked right out front. He motioned for them to go with him.

"How the hell did Evelyn get on the ranch?" Cameron hurried Lauren into the vehicle, and the moment they were in, Gabriel took off.

"We think she came in on that trail at the back of your house."

The one that Lauren had used. Lauren shook her

head, maybe to let him know that she hadn't told the woman about the trail, but her headshake wasn't necessary. Cameron knew she wouldn't do that.

"Here's the thing, though," Jodi continued a moment later. "There's no vehicle on the trail. The hands checked. When they found Evelyn, she was in your yard. She looks dazed or something. I think someone might have drugged her."

Well, hell. Cameron certainly hadn't expected that. "Was she armed?"

"No. And she has some cuts and scratches on her hands. They look like defensive wounds to me."

Cameron looked at Lauren to see if she was making sense of this, but she seemed just as baffled as he was. Maybe, though, this was some kind of ruse. Or trap.

That put his heart in his throat. "Are you outside with her?" he asked Jodi. Cameron met Gabriel's gaze in the rearview mirror and saw the concern in his eyes.

"Yes. The hands brought her here, but I didn't want her in the house."

Neither did Cameron. But he didn't want Gabriel's wife being gunned down. "Move her to the porch." It wasn't ideal, but at least it would give Jodi a little cover, and she wouldn't be so out in the open.

"Make sure the hands keep watch," Gabriel added. "We're already on the road and will be there soon."

"Hurry," Jodi said. "I got a bad feeling about this."

Since Lauren, Gabriel and he had been attacked

just hours earlier, Cameron wasn't feeling so easy, either. Of course, Evelyn usually brought trouble with her wherever she went.

Cameron ended the call so he could keep watch around them. After all, they were going to have to drive right past the place where Maria had been shot.

And where Lauren had killed a man.

It wouldn't be a good thing for her to see—since she'd be reliving that latest nightmare—but it was the shortest route to the ranch, and they would have to take it. The minutes counted now, and he wanted to get to Jodi so that she wouldn't have to be in harm's way. Judging from the way Gabriel was speeding, he felt the same.

"Why would Evelyn have done this?" Lauren said, but she seemed to be talking more to herself than to him.

"Maybe she's desperate." Or worse. She could have gone off the deep end.

Cameron's phone rang, the sound causing Lauren to gasp. It got Gabriel's attention, too. Probably because he thought it was his wife calling back with bad news. But it wasn't a number that Cameron recognized.

That bad feeling skyrocketed. Because this could be one of the gunmen. Cameron answered it, putting it on speaker, but he didn't say anything.

"Deputy Doran?" the caller asked. "I'm Judge Wendell Olsen. I'm a friend of Evelyn—"

"I know who you are," Cameron interrupted.

"Did you put her up to trespassing onto the Beckett Ranch?"

The judge made a slight gasping sound. "Trespassing? No, Evelyn wouldn't do that."

Cameron didn't groan, but that was what he wanted to do. "Yes, she would, and she's there now."

"Not by choice. Something must have happened."

Either that or the judge didn't know just how loony his friend could be. "Why are you calling?" Cameron didn't bother to make his tone sound even marginally pleasant because he didn't like this clueless clown distracting him.

"I was worried about Evelyn. And her housekeeper just called. SAPD found Evelyn's car in a parking lot at a bar in south San Antonio. It's not an area where Evelyn would go. I think she was kidnapped."

That would mesh with the defensive wounds that Jodi thought the woman might have. Still, Cameron wasn't buying this. Evelyn could have something up her sleeve.

"Why would a kidnapper take Evelyn to the ranch?" Cameron came out and asked the judge.

"To make her look guilty of violating her restraining order. And you're the person who'd gain the most from that." The judge also wasn't tossing out any friendly vibes.

It took Cameron a moment to get his jaw unclenched. "You just accused me of a felony. Want to rethink that?"

Silence. For a long time. "I don't want you rail-roading a woman who simply wants to see her grand-son."

"Evelyn doesn't want to *see* him," Cameron cor-rected. "She wants custody of him. Big difference, and from what I'm hearing, you think you're going to try to make that happen."

More silence from the judge. Then he said, "I'll get Evelyn's lawyer and the San Antonio cops out to the ranch."

"SAPD has no jurisdiction in Blue River," Cam-eron reminded him.

"Then I'll get the Rangers."

Olsen really wasn't going to like this. "No need. There's already one at the ranch. Jameson Beckett. I suppose you'll threaten us with the FBI next, but they have to be invited to an investigation. I'm not inviting them. Not for this anyway. However, I won-der what they would think about a judge pressuring local law enforcement to do his bidding because his friend with a criminal record just committed an-other crime."

Cameron figured that put a scowl on the judge's face. "I just want to make sure Evelyn's treated fairly." And with that, he ended the call.

Great. Now he had a meddling judge added to this mix. It made Cameron rethink the idea of stay-ing at the ranch. It was time for him to look into a safe house for Lauren and the babies.

Gabriel took the turn to the ranch so fast that

Cameron was surprised he didn't lose control of the cruiser. He grappled with the steering wheel, keeping it on the road, and he sped toward his house.

The hands were definitely out and about. Cameron spotted six of them, and one of them had to open the cattle gate so that Gabriel could drive through. The moment the house came into view, he saw the reserve deputy, Mark Clayton, in the front yard. And he also saw Jodi. She was indeed on the porch by the front door and was holding a gun. She had it aimed right at Evelyn, who was sitting on the top step a good eight feet away from Jodi.

Gabriel braked to a stop and threw open the door. In the same motion, he drew his gun. "Go inside," he told Jodi.

Cameron rarely heard that kind of emotion in his boss's voice, but it was definitely there now. Gabriel loved Jodi, and it was obvious he'd been worried about her. Cameron was, too, but he was just as concerned for Lauren and the others in the house.

"I told Jodi I'd keep an eye on the woman," Mark said, "but she insisted on doing it herself."

That didn't surprise Cameron. He'd known Jodi his whole life, and her stubborn streak was just as big as her heart. Since she was a security specialist, she had the training to hold someone at gunpoint. The training to protect herself, too, but Gabriel almost certainly hadn't wanted the woman he loved in danger.

"Wait inside with Jodi," Cameron told Lauren.

She hesitated, then shook her head. "I don't want Gabriel and you out here. It's too dangerous."

Lauren was right. A good sniper might be able to pick them off. That was why he had to hurry this along. He brushed a kiss on her cheek and gave her a nudge to get her moving. He gave her a different kind of nudge when he whispered, "Check on the boys. Make sure they're not near the windows."

Her eyes widened, and she practically ran inside. One down, one to go. Plus, he really did want to make sure the boys were in the safest place possible. Lauren would see to it that they were.

Gabriel, however, didn't go in. He went onto the porch, blocking the door with his body. Probably in case Evelyn tried to bolt inside.

"Your wife said she would shoot me if I moved," Evelyn told Gabriel.

"She would have. And if you move, I'll shoot you if Cameron doesn't beat me to it first."

It was an empty threat. Well, the shooting part was anyway. Jodi had told them that Evelyn wasn't armed, so they couldn't use deadly force on her, but Cameron would stop her if she tried to get in the house.

"Start talking," Cameron demanded. "Why are you here?"

Evelyn looked him straight in the eyes. "Because you set me up."

Cameron huffed and tried to rein in his temper. "Let's deal in reality and not fairy tales. I haven't had time to set you up. I've been too busy dodging bullets from hired guns. And if I did want to frame you for something, the ranch is the last place I'd bring you."

She kept staring at him as if trying to figure out if he was telling the truth. She must have decided he was because Evelyn finally looked away and touched her fingers to her mouth. The gesture muffled a sob. For the most part anyway. Cameron still heard it. Normally, he had a soft spot for a crying woman, but he wasn't feeling anything more than wariness when it came to Evelyn.

"Start from the beginning," Gabriel said. "Tell us what happened."

Since this could go on for a while and he was still in the yard, Cameron joined Gabriel by the door.

"I was leaving my office to go home when a cop pulled me over," Evelyn explained. "It wasn't a cop car, but he had a blue flashing light. And a badge. He showed me his badge." She pressed her fingers to her mouth again. "I lowered the window to ask him why he'd pulled me over, and he pulled a stun gun out. I fought him, but he hit me with it."

Evelyn turned, showing them her neck. There were indeed two wounds there that looked like the kind of marks a stun gun would make.

"Did you get the cop's name?" Gabriel asked.

"No. In fact, I don't remember much after the stun gun. I think he must have drugged me. When I woke up, I was out in the middle of nowhere. The woods," she clarified. "My car wasn't there. Neither was my phone or purse. So I started walking on a path. I ended up in your backyard."

"Convenient," Cameron mumbled.

She lifted her head, the anger flashing through her eyes. "No, it wasn't. I was attacked by a cop and brought here."

"By a fake cop," Cameron corrected. "Lauren, Duane and Julia all had fake police officers go to their homes. In Lauren's case, the guy shot her in the arm."

Evelyn gasped. "Was my grandson there when that happened?"

Cameron nodded. "He was in the house."

And he carefully watched Evelyn's expression. The color drained from her face, and she seemed horrified. But Cameron didn't know if that expression was because her grandson had been in danger or because Evelyn had hired those thugs and they'd gone against her order to make sure the baby was safe.

It took several moments before Evelyn regained her composure. "May I see him? May I see Patrick?"

Cameron didn't even have to think about this. "No. Not as long as you're a suspect in these attacks."

Even though that was a serious accusation he'd just made, Evelyn didn't lash out. "But you'd let me see him if there was no chance of his being in danger, if the fake cops and hired guns were caught?"

Now he had to think about it. "I'd consider it if I knew beyond a shadow of a doubt that you had no part in any of this. That includes Maria Black's murder."

Her mouth dropped open, and she got to her feet. "Maria's dead?"

Cameron wasn't going to get into how she knew the nurse. Apparently, everyone connected to this had known her.

"She's dead," Gabriel verified. "A gunshot wound to the chest at point-blank range. My guess is a fake cop who someone hired did that to her."

Evelyn shook her head and looked genuinely distressed about that. She glanced around as if trying to figure out what to do. Cameron hoped she didn't try to run because he didn't want to have to go after her.

"Will you be taking me to the sheriff's office?" she asked Gabriel.

Gabriel tipped his head to Mark. "No, he will be." He motioned toward Allen Colley, one of the hands who was close to the house. "And he'll go with you, too. I'll be there later when I've made sure things are okay here."

Both Cameron and Gabriel waited on the porch until Mark, Allen and Evelyn were in the cruiser and Mark had driven away.

"You believe her?" Gabriel asked him as they went inside.

"No." But then Cameron had to shrug. "Maybe she's telling the truth. Julia or Duane could have set her up because they needed a patsy." And Evelyn would have made a great patsy because of her police record.

Lauren and Jodi were right there waiting in the

foyer for them. Gabriel reset the security system, hooked his arm around Jodi and moved her away from the door. They went toward Gabriel's office.

"I heard most of what Evelyn said," Lauren volunteered. "First, though, I checked on the boys. They're okay."

Cameron didn't doubt that, but he wanted to see for himself so he made his way to the nursery. The relief came when he spotted them napping on a quilt on the floor. The disappointment, too, because he'd wanted to hold them. He certainly needed something to ease the tension he was feeling.

Lauren helped with that when she gave his hand a gentle squeeze.

Both Dara and Merilee were in the room, sitting on the floor next to the boys. The curtains were drawn, and the lights were off.

"Everything should be all right now," Cameron told them, and he hoped that was true.

Merilee gave a shaky nod and made her way to a chair where she picked up her e-reader. Dara said something about getting a snack and headed to the kitchen. He doubted she'd be eating, though, since she didn't look very steady.

Cameron hated what this was doing to Dara and Merilee. Hated what it was doing to all of them. Thankfully, the only ones who didn't seem to be aware of the danger were Patrick and Isaac.

He looked at Lauren, taking her back into the hall

so their conversation wouldn't wake the boys. But Lauren spoke before he had a chance to say anything.

"We're leaving the ranch?" she asked.

They were obviously on the same wavelength. He nodded. "It'll take me a while to set up a safe house, but I should have it ready by tomorrow."

She didn't question that. Didn't argue. But then, Lauren knew full well that the hired guns were still at large, and another attack could happen despite all their security measures.

"We'll also need to postpone the marriage plans," Cameron continued. "I don't want to take you back into town, and I don't think it's a smart idea to have the justice of the peace come here."

Lauren made a sound of agreement. "The thugs could maybe use him to get to us."

Yep. Heck, the thugs could use anyone, and that was why it was best if they were away from here. Every minute they stayed at the ranch, they put Lauren's family and the ranch hands in danger.

Cameron was about to find a quiet place to work so he could start on making the arrangements for the safe house, but he heard footsteps, and a moment later Jameson came into the hall. He looked in on the boys before he motioned for them to follow him into the foyer.

"I got some news on the loan shark Julia owes," Jameson explained. "The guy's name is Artie Tisdale, and he's bad news. He wouldn't say much to me on the phone. I think he was afraid I was recording it, but one of the other Rangers is headed over there now to talk to him."

It didn't surprise Cameron one bit that the guy was wary of talking to law enforcement. He probably wouldn't say much to the other Ranger, either, but they had to try.

"Did he admit Julia owed him money?" Lauren asked her brother.

"He chose his words carefully, said that he'd *helped Julia out* when she was short of cash, but of course he didn't admit to being a loan shark. He also didn't say anything about what he would do if Julia didn't pay back the cash soon."

Cameron thought about that. "Tisdale could have paid for the hired guns. Heck, they could be on his payroll. Is there anything to link Tisdale to the dead gunmen?"

"There's no money trail, but yeah, I could see Tisdale doing that to protect his investment. If Julia gets her brother's estate, then she could pay back Tisdale's loan along with all his other expenses."

Lauren shuddered, rubbing her hands along the sides of her arms. She winced a little, too. A reminder of her injury. Cameron wanted to kick himself for not having a medic check her out when they'd been at the sheriff's office.

"I'll let you know if the Ranger gets anything more from Tisdale," Jameson went on. "In the meantime, I'll look for any connection between Tisdale and the thugs. Something might turn up."

Cameron wanted that to happen, but a loan shark had probably covered his tracks.

Jameson turned to walk away, but Gabriel came hurrying into the foyer. One look at his face, and Cameron knew something was wrong.

"Please tell me there aren't gunmen on the ranch," Lauren said.

Gabriel shook his head. "No, but gunmen just attacked Allen and Mark. And they took Evelyn."

Chapter Thirteen

Lauren stared out the window of the guest room. She wasn't standing directly in front of it, though. Cameron's orders. He'd also told her to keep the curtains shut, which she had, but she could still look out through the small gap on the side where the curtains met the wall. She could see part of the ranch and her parents' old house.

It was a view she'd seen a lot as a kid since Gabriel's place had once belonged to their grandparents.

She'd come here plenty of times and stayed in the rambling big house. Had actually stayed in this very room even though in those days it had been her gran's sewing room. But this was a first for her to stand at the window and keep watch for hired guns.

And Evelyn.

Everyone was on the lookout for the woman. For the thugs, too. But the ranch had over a thousand acres. That made it nearly impossible to watch every part of it. The gunmen could take advantage of that. Maybe Evelyn, too.

Since that only caused Lauren to feel more depressed, she turned her attention to the makeshift bed on the floor where the boys were sleeping. Dara and Merilee had volunteered to sleep in the nursery with them, but Lauren had thought it was safer for them to be on the second floor. Plus, she hadn't wanted them near her. That way, if something went wrong, she could grab them and try to escape.

At least Mark and Allen hadn't been hurt when the gunmen had attacked the cruiser. In fact, Mark had said the men hadn't even seemed interested in them. The goons had rammed into the cruiser, running it off the road. When that happened, they'd opened the door, dragged out Evelyn and put the woman in their SUV before they sped away.

Lauren had no idea if Evelyn was still alive or if this had been some ruse to make it look as if she'd been taken. Either was possible. Heck, the judge could have even helped her do this so she could escape.

Lauren sank down on the floor not far from the boys, and she leaned the back of her head against the bed. Her body needed sleep, but her mind was still racing too much for that to happen. Maybe, though, she'd be able to get in a nap since they would likely be moving to the safe house in the morning. That would bring a whole new set of worries since they'd have to take the boys out in the open, but maybe once they were in place, there'd be some peace of mind, too.

All of their suspects and the hired guns knew the location of the ranch. They almost certainly knew Cameron, the boys and she were in Gabriel's house. That was why they had to move, and Lauren only wished they didn't have to go through the long night before that happened.

She'd left the door open, so she had no trouble hearing someone walking toward the bedroom. It was Cameron. Not a surprise. He'd been checking on them and giving her updates every half hour or so. Since he'd been keeping his footsteps light—hard to do with cowboy boots on a wood floor—he probably hoped that he would find her asleep. At least the boys were, and that was enough for now.

Even though the lights were all off, there was still enough illumination coming from downstairs that she could see his weary expression. Of course, that weary expression was on a very hot face, so she saw that, as well. As she usually did when she had eyes on Cameron, she felt that tug in her belly. Felt it lower, too. But she figured they were both way too tired for tugs or kisses.

"Anything on Evelyn?" she whispered. Best to get her mind on something else other than Cameron's face.

He shook his head, went to her and sank down next to her on the floor. Not touching her exactly, but he sat close enough for her to catch his scent. He'd showered, probably because he'd had blood on his shirt from the earlier attack. Now he was not only wearing clean clothes, he also smelled like soap and the leather from his boots.

That didn't help the tug.

Normally, she wouldn't have considered those scents a turn-on, but her body suddenly seemed very interested in that combination.

"There's been no ransom demand," Cameron said. "And she hasn't turned up dead. Judge Olsen thinks we're behind it, of course. I think Evelyn wants to play the victim card because she thinks it might stop her from being arrested. It won't," Cameron assured her.

Good. Well, maybe good. If Evelyn was guilty, Lauren definitely wanted her in jail, but the truth was, the woman could be a pawn in all of this. A pawn who could now be in grave danger if those thugs weren't actually working for her.

"Gabriel did find out more on the cooked books that Julia claims she found," Cameron went on. "There's definitely some money missing from the accounts. Not a lot, considering the company has over ten million in assets." He turned to her. "Did you know it was worth that much?"

She nodded. "Isaac is the heir to all of that."

He stayed quiet a moment, a muscle flexing in his cheek. "I'd give away every penny to keep him safe."

So would she—along with every cent in her own personal accounts. But even that wouldn't ensure he was safe. Those thugs could still come after them.

"How much money was missing?" she asked.

"About thirty grand. Enough to fund the attacks and then some."

Yes, it was. "I'm guessing Duane is saying he's innocent, that he didn't take it?"

He nodded, but his forehead bunched up when he looked down at her. Not her face. But her shoulder. Cameron mumbled some profanity, reached out and unbuttoned her shirt. Since this didn't seem to be his version of hasty foreplay, Lauren figured he was checking her wound.

"I meant to change the bandage for you," he said, peeling it back and having a look at it.

She'd already had a look, and while the sight of it turned her stomach, it wasn't serious. "I changed it after my shower," she told him. "Jodi gave me some antibiotic cream to use on it."

He made a sound, sort of a disapproving grunt. Maybe because the wound turned his stomach, too. Or maybe he thought the home doctoring wasn't nearly enough.

Since he was examining her, Lauren did the same to him. She eased back the bandage on his forehead and had a look. It was clean but would probably leave a scar. It would just give him some more character on his face.

As if Cameron needed more of that.

"You're scowling," he pointed out. "Does the cut look that bad?"

She lowered her gaze, making eye contact with him, and Lauren wasn't sure what he saw, but the corner of his mouth lifted for a moment. "Oh, *that*," he said.

Yes, that. She looked away, but it didn't help. She was already caught up in the moment. Lauren would have liked to blame it on spent adrenaline and the fact that she didn't know if she was going to live long enough to see another day. Realizing something like that had a way of making every moment seem as if it might be her last. But she couldn't lie to herself. What she was feeling had to do with the attraction and nothing else.

"I kissed you in this room once," he said, glancing around.

He had, and she was a little surprised he remembered. She'd been seventeen then. Her grandparents had already passed away and Gabriel had moved in. Lauren had come to get her gran's sewing machine so she could mend the seam on her favorite shirt. Cameron had walked with her there so he could help her carry it back to her house.

"Apparently, a chore like that was fuel for a kiss back then," she joked.

"Breathing was fuel for a kiss," he joked back.

Except it was the truth. Still was. And that caused Lauren to sigh.

She should just get up, move away from him and keep watch again. There were so many reasons for her not to be with him. She didn't want it to cloud her mind. She shouldn't jump into that kind of intimacy until she was certain of her feelings for him. Plus, the boys were in the room.

But those good reasons turned to dust when Cameron leaned in and kissed her.

Despite his being so close, she hadn't seen the kiss coming, but Lauren had no trouble feeling it. One touch from his mouth, and the heat trickled through her. Head to toe.

He lingered a moment, deepening the kiss, before he pulled back and looked at her. Maybe to gauge her reaction. It must have gauged well because it caused him to give that hot half smile again.

"I guess breathing is still a fuel," he said, his voice low. Husky. A Texas drawl that pulled her right in.

Lauren figured either walking out or staying would be the wrong thing to do. Staying would lead to sex. Walking out would no doubt give her plenty of regrets. That was why she slid her hand around the back of Cameron's neck and pulled him to her for another kiss.

And she made sure it was plenty long and deep.

Enough to rid them of the breath that was apparently fueling some of this. Of course, the kiss did its own share of fueling, too.

"Give yourself some time. Think about it before you do anything," she said.

Cameron looked up at her, and she had no trouble seeing the surprise on his face. Lauren figured that surprise increased a lot more when she got to her feet and headed for the door.

CAMERON WASN'T SURE what was going on in Lauren's head, but he sure as heck knew what was going on in the rest of her. That'd been heat he'd seen in her eyes. Plenty of it. And the heat had been in her kiss, too.

So why was she leaving?

The simple answer to that was she wasn't, and he would make certain of that. He got up as fast as he could and hurried to her. She'd already made it into the hall by the time he caught up with her, but she was just standing there—as if trying to figure out what to do.

"Is this about having second thoughts?" he asked.

A soft breath left her mouth. "No. Second thoughts happened hours ago. I'm on third and fourth thoughts now."

Yeah, he'd been there, done that. And all those doubts hadn't solved a thing. He still wanted Lauren, and she felt the same way about him. Cameron proved that in a really stupid way. He hooked his arm around her waist, hauled her to him and kissed her.

Obviously, if Lauren needed some thinking time, this was not the way to go about it. So he didn't kiss her for long. Just enough to rid her of more of her breath. And he stepped back. Cameron figured she was either about to chew him out or—

She went with the *or*.

She took hold of the front of his shirt, gathering it up in her hand as she pulled him closer. Lauren kissed him, and this time it wasn't a kiss to prove anything. It was scalding hot and meant to send them straight to bed.

Cameron responded, all right. He put his arms around her, dragging her right against him. Not that it took much effort. Lauren was already headed in that direction. Her breasts landed on his chest while the kiss raged on.

Cameron did his own version of raging. He slid his hand beneath her top, touching the bare skin on her stomach. It was hard to think, but he forced himself to remember the gunshot wound on her shoulder. He didn't want to hurt her.

If the injury was bothering her, Lauren showed no signs of it. She also showed no signs of the timid teenager who'd become his lover over ten years ago. No. This was a woman's kiss. A woman's touch. And this woman apparently knew exactly what she wanted.

She wanted him.

Lauren turned him, putting his back to the wall, holding him in place while she made the kiss even deeper. Cameron did more touching, too, sliding his hands into the cups of her bra. She must have liked that because she made a sound of pleasure. It wasn't loud, but it gave him another reminder.

They were in the hall of her brother's house. Gabriel or the others could come walking up at any second.

Cameron silently cursed and started maneuvering her back into the bedroom so he could shut the door. Of course, there was a problem here, too. The babies. Yeah, they were asleep, but if much more moaning and grappling went on, Lauren and he could wake them.

When he stopped kissing her, Lauren looked to see what'd caught his attention. She glanced at the boys. Then, back at Cameron. All the while she was nibbling on her bottom lip. Maybe she was realizing the logistics of having sex wasn't going to be easy.

But it wasn't impossible.

Cameron looped his arm around her and got her moving. He grabbed the baby monitor along the way but put it on the counter as soon as they were in the adjoining bathroom. Lauren was the one who shut the door, and she immediately launched into another kiss.

The overhead light was off, and Cameron kept it that way, though there was a night-light by the sink. It was just enough for him to see the heat and the determined look in her eyes.

He was still having doubts about whether this should happen or not, but the longer the kiss went on, the more the doubts faded. Soon, he quit thinking and went with it. He pulled Lauren back to him, and this time he had more than kissing on his mind. Well, more than just kissing her mouth anyway.

She made another of those pleasure sounds when Cameron pushed up her top and kissed her breasts through the lace cups of her bra. It was good, but it got a whole lot better when he opened the front clip.

That way, he could kiss her without the thin layer of fabric between them. She must have liked that, as well, because she fisted her hand in his hair and held on.

As he went lower.

Cameron got in some kisses to her stomach. Got her unzipped, as well, but Lauren seemed to want to kick up the pace. She achieved that by sliding her hand down into the waist of his jeans.

Yeah, she was kicking this up, all right.

He got rock-hard. And desperate to have her. Not exactly a good combination when he needed to make sure he didn't hurt her while he also listened to the baby monitor.

"Please tell me you have a condom," she said.

"Wallet, back pocket," he managed to answer.

She went after it, doing some clever touching along the way. It felt more like foreplay than looking for something they needed for safe sex. Of course, there were a lot of other "unsafe" things about this, but Cameron chose not to think about that right now. That probably had plenty to do with Lauren unzipping him.

Since there wasn't exactly anywhere else to go, Cameron lowered her to the floor. His back landed on the hard tile, but he barely noticed.

That was because Lauren landed on him.

Straddling him, she took out the condom and tossed his wallet aside.

Cameron did a little tossing, too. Even though he

liked seeing Lauren on top of him, he had to move her to get her out of those jeans. Not easy to do. The bathroom wasn't that big, and Lauren wasn't making things easier because she was fighting to get his jeans off, too.

Everything suddenly felt way too urgent, and it was taking an eternity to rid them of their clothes. Cameron finally managed it, and Lauren moved back on top again. It was the best position so that her shoulder didn't get hurt, though he certainly didn't see any trace of pain on her face.

But he did see the pleasure.

Cameron was certain there was plenty of that on his face, too, because he was feeling a whole lot of it in his body. The feeling went up significantly when she got the condom on him and took him inside her.

Lauren went still, as if savoring this for a moment, and in the milky light, she made eye contact with him. It was as if the past ten years just vanished. They were young lovers again before the tragedy that had torn them apart. The ache came. The reminder of just how much he'd lost that night.

And then it was gone.

Because Lauren started to move. That rid him of the ache but created a different kind of one. His need to pleasure her. The need for release.

He caught on to her hips, guiding the movement that was taking him in and out of her. Not that she needed any guidance. Lauren was doing just fine on her own. Better than fine, actually. She was taking them both to the only place that either of them wanted to go.

She put her hands on his chest, anchoring herself while she leaned down and kissed him. Her mouth was still on his when she pushed against him one last time and shattered. That was all Cameron needed, and with the taste of her roaring through him, he gave in to the release and went with her.

Chapter Fourteen

The sound woke Lauren, and she jackknifed in the bed. It was a loud boom. And for several heart-stopping moments, she thought they were under attack, that one of those hired thugs had made it onto the ranch and fired a shot at them.

"A storm moved in," Cameron said. He was close to the bed. Very close. Right by the nightstand just a couple of inches from her. "It's thunder."

She heard the words, but it took a while for them to register. It was indeed storming. Lauren could hear the rain hitting against the windows and the tin roof. There was even a crack of lightning. But she wasn't sure how she'd managed to sleep through that or Cameron getting out of the bed.

Actually, she wasn't sure how she'd managed to sleep at all.

She had, though. She had apparently fallen asleep after Cameron carried her to the bed, and now it was morning. *Late* morning. Well, late for her anyway. It was seven thirty.

"I took the boys downstairs when they woke up about a half hour ago," Cameron said as he made an adjustment to his shoulder holster. "Dara and Merilee changed them and are feeding them breakfast."

Good grief. She'd slept through the babies getting up, as well. Obviously, sex with Cameron was an amazing stress reliever for her to be able to do that. She hadn't slept through the night since she'd become a mother.

"You should have gotten me up sooner," she grumbled.

He shrugged. "I had some things I had to work out. Things to do with the investigation," he added. "Besides, I wanted you to get some rest."

She wanted him to have some rest, too, but she was betting he hadn't gotten much. They'd gotten in bed together, but before she'd fallen into a deep sleep, she'd remembered him getting up to go to the window to look out. Keeping watch to make sure those thugs didn't come back for another round.

She threw back the covers, only to remember that she was stark naked. Cameron noticed, too, and he gave her one of those lazy smiles that reminded her of why she'd landed on the bathroom floor with him in the first place.

"We need to talk, so you should probably get dressed."

"Talk?" she questioned.

"About the safe house. About some other things." He was obviously keeping it vague, and she might have pressed for more, but he leaned down, brushing a kiss on her mouth. Coming from any other man, it would have qualified as a peck, but even a brief kiss was potent when it came from Cameron.

"I'll meet you in the kitchen," he added and headed for the door. But then he stopped and looked back at her. "By the way, Gabriel knows we were together last night. He came to the room at around five to check on you."

Lauren groaned. She didn't mind Gabriel knowing, but it wasn't something she wanted to discuss with him. Gabriel wouldn't feel the same way, though. She'd get another big-brother lecture from him about guarding her heart.

And it was a lecture she needed to hear.

She should do some heart-guarding, but considering she'd had sex with Cameron—amazing sex at that—that ship had already sailed.

The moment Cameron was out of the room and had shut the door, Lauren hurried from the bed and to the shower. She didn't even wait for the water to reach the right temperature. She just rushed through it and tried not to think of what could go wrong with the move to the safe house. They'd already been through so much, and she didn't want anything else bad to happen.

Lauren changed her bandage, got dressed and was ready to rush out of the room when she spotted something on the floor to the side of the vanity. Cameron's wallet. She'd tossed it there after she'd taken out the condom, and Cameron must not have seen it. She picked it up, the wallet falling open. And that was when she saw it.

The edge of the photo.

It was tucked in one of the slots normally used for credit cards. Without thinking, she lifted it out and got a shock. It was a picture of Cameron and her. They were smiling, and he had his arm slung over her shoulders.

She instantly remembered when it'd been taken. They'd been outside the barn at her house, and Ivy had just walked in on them making out. They'd been fully clothed, thank goodness, but Ivy had insisted on snapping the shot with her phone. Her sister had sent them both the picture, but Cameron must have had his printed out.

Strange that he would have kept it all these years. It seemed like something a man would do when he was in love, and Cameron had never come close to saying the L-word to her. Of course, maybe he'd put the photo there way back then and had forgotten about it.

Lauren headed downstairs, hoping to find Cameron alone so that she could give him the wallet without anyone noticing. No such luck. He was in the kitchen and so was everyone else who was staying in the house.

Like all the other rooms, the curtains and blinds were drawn here. Merilee and Dara were at the table eating breakfast. Jameson was holding Patrick, and

Cameron had Isaac. Jodi was at the back window, peering out the side of the blinds. And Cameron and Gabriel were going over a map that was on the laptop computer screen.

They all stopped what they were doing and looked at her.

Gabriel's eyebrow lifted, and since it seemed as if everyone in the room knew what had happened in the guest room bath, she went to Cameron, kissed his cheek and handed him his wallet. What he didn't do was smile or kiss her back. For a moment she thought that was because Gabriel was standing there, but everyone else was looking somber, as well.

"What happened?" Lauren immediately asked.

Cameron put his wallet in his pocket and touched the map. That was when Lauren realized it wasn't an ordinary map. It was the ranch. It showed not only some of the trails but also the nearby roads.

"About two hours ago, one of the hands spotted a suspicious vehicle here. A black SUV." Cameron tapped the road that was only about a quarter of a mile from Gabriel's house. "The hands were down by the cattle gate and used binoculars to read the license plate." He paused. "It was bogus. There's no vehicle registered with those plate numbers."

Well, there went any trace of that dreamy morning-after feel from sex. Lauren glanced at the others and realized they'd already learned this bad news. And it was bad. That vehicle had been way too close to the house. Obviously, this is what Cameron had meant by needing to talk to her, but Lauren had figured it was going to be a discussion about arrangements for the safe house.

"Two hours," she repeated. "Why didn't you come up and wake me?"

"I woke Cameron instead," Gabriel said, looking straight at her.

Good grief. She wasn't normally such a sound sleeper, but that did explain why they'd had the time to come up with this plan. They'd probably been talking about it for the past two hours, and that meant Cameron hadn't just rolled out of bed when she'd awakened. He'd probably come up just so he could have her get dressed.

There was a loud boom of thunder, and Patrick started to fuss. Lauren took him, cuddling him close to her and hoping he didn't pick up on the fear that was starting to crawl through her.

"The SUV was gone by the time I made it to the road," Jameson said, obviously taking up where Cameron had left off. "I looked around but didn't see it."

What he didn't say was that didn't mean it was gone. The SUV could be on one of the trails or a side road.

"I have a reserve deputy posted here." Gabriel tapped the road that led from town to the ranch. "About an hour ago he saw a black SUV. It had different license plates from the one that was near here.

But the plates were fake, too. The deputy went in pursuit, but the vehicle got onto the main highway before he could reach it."

If there were hired thugs in the second SUV, they could have doubled back. Or while the deputy was out chasing them, more hired guns could have gotten in place to launch an attack. That spelled out the bottom line for Lauren.

"It's too risky to take the babies out on the road," she said. "We can't take them to a safe house."

Gabriel, Jodi and Jameson all made sounds of agreement. Cameron groaned. "That doesn't mean they'll be safe here, either. You saw how easily Evelyn got through the trails. So could these guys."

That panic and fear weren't just crawling now. Both emotions were at a full sprint. Their situation sounded hopeless, but it couldn't be. They couldn't just stand by waiting for another attack.

"We need to do something." Lauren knew she sounded desperate because she was.

Cameron nodded, then paused. He looked as if he wanted to curse. "I don't like even asking you to do this, but I can't think of another way. Our first priority has to be to keep the babies safe."

"I agree," Lauren said without hesitation. "What do we need to do?"

Cameron looked her straight in the eyes. "We're going to have to force the gunmen to come after us. We'll have to make ourselves bait."

"FOR THE RECORD, I don't like this plan," Gabriel spat out.

Neither did Cameron, but he couldn't stomach the thought of the babies being caught up in another attack. Apparently, neither could Lauren.

"So, how do we do this?" she asked. Again, no hesitation. "How soon can we make it happen?"

She probably had doubts, just as Cameron and Gabriel did, but Cameron knew something that was much worse than doubts and fear, and that was having the babies they loved in danger.

"The cruiser is already parked out front," Cameron explained. "You and I will pretend to get into it with the babies. What we'll be carrying are blankets that will hopefully look as if we have the boys. Since it's pouring rain, it shouldn't seem suspicious that we'd have them covered up like that."

"Where will the babies be?" Lauren asked him. Patrick was still fussing a little so she rocked him gently, brushing a kiss on the top of his head.

"Patrick and Isaac will stay here at the house with Gabriel, Jodi, the nannies and Mark, the reserve deputy. Jameson and Jace will come with you and me."

Cameron took a deep breath before he continued. Here was the part that was going to make Lauren very uneasy. "The gunmen probably have the place under surveillance, so we need to make them believe the babies are truly gone from the ranch. That means sending the hands back to the bunkhouse and to the barns. We need them out of sight."

She shook her head. "But what if gunmen come here after we leave?"

That was a question that had bothered Cameron right after he'd learned about the SUV being in the area. "The ranch hands will be close enough to respond." Not immediately, though. And that in itself was a risk.

"Merilee and Dara will be in the hall bathroom with the boys," Gabriel added. "It's the safest place in the house since there are no windows. Jodi, Mark and I will stand guard. If there's a sign of trouble, we'll sound the alarm and get all of you back here."

And there was the other concern that was eating away at Cameron. If there was trouble, then Lauren and he could be right in the line of fire. That was better than having the babies at risk, but it was nowhere near ideal.

Simply put, Lauren could be hurt.

Heck, Jace and Jameson could be, too.

"If we see the SUV once we're on the road," Cameron continued, "then it'll almost certainly follow us. We'll lead them here." He pointed to one of the larger trails that was about five miles from Gabriel's house. "Or here." Cameron moved his finger to another trail. "It's far enough away from the ranch—"

"Wait," Lauren interrupted. "Why lead them there? There are woods. The river, even."

"There'll be some hands, reserve deputies and even Rangers hidden on those trails." He checked his watch. "They'll be in place by now."

And with some luck, the hired guns hadn't spotted them. If they had...well, Cameron didn't want to go there.

"We also recorded this shortly before you came downstairs." Jameson hit a button on his phone to play the sound of the baby whimpering. It was almost identical to what Patrick had been doing just moments earlier, but this had come from Isaac when Merilee had stopped him from spilling his sippy cup of milk.

"Why would you need that?" she asked, turning first to Jameson and then to Cameron.

"In case the attackers call us." Cameron patted his phone. "They have my number because they've called me before. This way, they'll hear the recording and believe the babies are with us."

Lauren stood there, her forehead bunched up. She was obviously processing all of this, and Cameron wished he could give her more time, but he couldn't.

"If you can think of a safer way to do this," Cameron said to her, "I'd love to hear it."

Lauren rocked Patrick some more and shook her head. "Would we leave now?"

Cameron nodded. "The sooner the better. We need to put some distance between the boys and us."

She blew out a breath, kissed Patrick again and then did the same to Isaac. Lauren handed Patrick to Dara. "Please take care of them," she whispered, and she included Gabriel and Jodi in the glances she gave the nannies.

"I'll get the blankets ready," Jodi said, passing Isaac to Merilee. She headed out of the room.

Gabriel handed Lauren a gun that he took from the top of the fridge, and she tucked it in the back waistband of her jeans. "I've already given Cameron some extra ammo," Gabriel explained. "And make sure your phone is with you. Just in case."

Yeah, in case this plan went south and those goons tried to kill them. If that happened, then Lauren would be the one who'd probably have to make the call since Jameson, Jace and he would be returning fire.

Lauren checked to make sure, and she already had her phone in her front pocket. That meant they were as ready as they could be.

Jameson certainly didn't seem so eager to get out the door. He huffed and grabbed two Kevlar vests that he'd gotten from Gabriel's home office. "My advice is to lay this on top of the blankets. So it looks as if you're protecting the babies. Then, once you're in the cruiser, put them on." He tapped his chest. "Jace and I are already wearing ours."

That was something Jace and Jameson had done because they'd thought they would be taking the babies to the safe house. Now they would be doing backup for Lauren and him, and the vests might come in handy.

It didn't take Jodi long to return with the blankets, and she'd already rolled them up in such a way that it did look like bundled babies. She handed one to each of them, and while Lauren took it, holding it against her shoulder as she'd done to Patrick, she also gave both boys another kiss.

Cameron kissed them, too, and he draped the vests over the blanket bundles, but he didn't linger. "Go ahead and take them to the bathroom," Cameron instructed the nannies.

No need to stretch out this goodbye. For one thing, it wasn't the safe thing to do, and besides, there were tears in Lauren's eyes. Best not to have her break down. Not until they were in the cruiser, at least.

Cameron waited until he heard the bathroom door shut with the nannies and the boys inside, and Jameson, Lauren and he headed to the front door where Jace was waiting.

"Move fast," Gabriel instructed.

Lauren probably hadn't needed anything else to put more alarm in her eyes, but that did it. Because it was a reminder that there could be snipers.

Gabriel turned off the security system so they could get out the door, but Cameron was certain he would reset it. There wasn't anyone else he trusted more to protect Patrick and Isaac, but Cameron prayed it would be enough.

The rain seemed to be coming down harder now, and the lightning was close. So close that the thunder boomed almost immediately after the strikes. Definitely not a good time to be out driving, but they couldn't wait it out. The storm was supposed to last most of the day.

Cameron took hold of Lauren's arm to help her down the slippery steps, and Jace and Jameson ran ahead of them to open the doors. The moment they were inside, Jace drove away.

Lauren looked back at the house, tears watering her eyes, and even though Cameron doubted it would help, he kissed her. Her gaze came to his then, and even though she didn't say anything, he knew her heart was breaking.

She'd been through way too much in the past couple of days, and he certainly hadn't helped matters by having sex with her. Yeah, it'd felt necessary at the time, but it had caused them both to lose focus. Had been confusing, as well. But that was something he could dwell on another time.

"Go ahead and put on the vest," Cameron instructed.

He lay the blankets on the seat next to her and helped her into the Kevlar before she put on her seat belt. Cameron got on both his jacket and his seat belt, and then he immediately drew his gun. That didn't help with the alarm in Lauren's eyes, either.

"It's just a precaution," he told her. A necessary one.

As they'd discussed, Jace drove away from town and in the direction of one of the trails. It was hard to see much of anything because of the rain sheeting over the windows. Still, Cameron kept watch. So did Jameson and Jace from the front seat.

"So what's put Gabriel in a snit?" Jameson asked. He glanced back at his sister. "And it's not a snit because of the danger. I'm pretty sure this one's more personal."

Lauren frowned. "Gabriel found me with Cameron."

Jameson laughed. "Like old times. I seem to remember him not approving of you two way back when."

He hadn't. Gabriel had thought Cameron was too old for Lauren. And he had been. But that age difference no longer seemed like an obstacle. A good thing, too, because they had plenty of other obstacles to get in their way.

"Want my advice?" Jameson said, but he didn't wait for Lauren to answer. "Just let Gabriel know you're in love with Cameron, and he'll back off. Love cures a lot of ill will between siblings."

Lauren made a sound of surprise that was borderline outrage. That meant she didn't love him. Not that he thought she did. Lauren had fallen out of love with him years ago, and heck, it probably hadn't even been real love then. He'd been her crush.

A thought that made him frown.

Was that all it'd been?

The attraction had definitely been there, now and then. But maybe her feelings for him hadn't gone beyond basic lust.

"You were more than a crush to me," Cameron mumbled under his breath, but it was obviously loud enough for Lauren to hear because she practically snapped toward him.

However, she didn't blurt out anything to reassure him that he'd just babbled the truth. "You have a picture of us in your wallet," she said.

Now she was the one who looked alarmed at saying something she hadn't meant to say. He nodded, admitting that he did indeed have a picture. One she must have seen when he'd left his wallet on the bathroom floor. But Cameron didn't get a chance to add anything to his nod. That was because Jameson spoke first.

"A black SUV just pulled out of the side road behind us." Jameson drew his gun and turned in the seat. "And it's following us."

Chapter Fifteen

The plan was working. Now Lauren had to hope that was a good thing and that they could truly lead these thugs away from the ranch.

"Speed up," Cameron instructed Jace. "They'd expect us to do that if we actually had the babies in the car."

Cameron gave an uneasy glance behind them at the SUV, followed by an equally uneasy one at the sky. Going fast on these roads wasn't a safe idea, but he was right. They needed to make this as realistic as possible. That meant taking risks.

More than the ones they'd already taken.

She prayed that whatever they would do, it would make Patrick and Isaac safe. Lauren didn't want these goons anywhere near the boys. Still, it was a chance that could happen. While Cameron and she were luring the gunmen, the gunmen could be playing a cat-and-mouse game to get them away from the house.

"They're speeding up, too," Jace relayed.

Lauren got a glimpse of that, and yes, the SUV was much closer now, but Cameron took hold of her arm and lowered her to the seat. "Pick up the blankets," he instructed. "Hold them as if you'd be holding the boys. The cruiser windows are tinted, but they still might be able to see inside."

True, and again they had to make this look believable. Lauren gathered up the blankets in her arms, making sure they stayed rolled up.

"How much farther is the trail where we'll be turning?" she asked.

Cameron didn't jump to answer, and she saw the renewed alarm on his face. "Hold on," he warned her. "They're going to hit us."

It wasn't a second too soon because the jolt came. So hard that even with her seat belt on, it slung her forward. The strap caught her wounded shoulder in the wrong place and caused the pain to shoot through her. She made a sharp gasp that she tried to muffle, but she failed because Cameron looked at her. But he didn't look for long.

That was because the SUV rammed into them again.

The cruiser went into a skid on the wet pavement, and she could see Jace fighting with the steering wheel to keep control. The cruiser tires clipped the gravel area just off the asphalt and sent a spray of rocks banging against the doors and undercarriage. It sounded like gunfire.

"Hold on," Cameron repeated, and this time he took hold of her.

The SUV rammed into them again. And again. Obviously, the front end of the vehicle had been reinforced because the engine was still roaring behind them.

"Let me see if I can do something about this," Cameron said when Jace finally got the cruiser back on the road surface.

He lowered his window, the rain immediately dampening the backseat. Despite the summer temperatures, the spray of water was cold, and Lauren started to shiver. Part of the shivering, however, was because Cameron was about to make himself an easy target for those hired killers.

Cameron leaned out enough so he could take aim, and he sent two shots in the direction of the SUV. Since Lauren was down on the seat, she couldn't tell if he hit anything, but at least the SUV didn't ram into them.

But the gunmen did something worse.

They returned fire. The shots slammed into the roof of the cruiser. The bullets didn't tear through it, but Lauren could hear them slice across the metal.

"Why would they be shooting with the babies inside?" she asked, the question meant more for herself than the others. "Why would they risk that?" It didn't make sense if they wanted the boys alive.

If.

"They're not firing kill shots," Cameron answered.

"If they were, they'd be shooting into the window. I think they're just trying to run us off the road."

Yes, but even that could hurt Patrick and Isaac. Maybe that meant these thugs didn't care if the babies were harmed or not. Or they could have figured out the boys weren't in the cruiser.

That thought didn't make her breathe any easier.

Lauren tried not to panic, but it was hard to rein in the fear. Not only were their precious babies in danger, but these goons could end up killing Cameron and her in a car wreck, too. Of course, that could be what the person behind this wanted. If it was Julia or Duane, they wanted her dead. Evelyn probably felt the same way about Cameron. She didn't want to think of what would happen to Patrick and Isaac if these thugs succeeded in carrying out whatever orders they had.

"How long before we get to the trail?" Lauren repeated.

"A minute, maybe." Jace was volleying glances between the road and the rearview mirror.

The SUV rammed into them once more, but this time Jace managed to keep control. There was no other traffic, thank goodness, so Jace swerved into the oncoming lane to stop them from being hit again.

"Let me try to hold them off." Jameson lowered his window as Cameron had done, and he sent three shots at the SUV.

Maybe those shots would buy them some seconds until they could get to the trail. Of course, the SUV would follow them. That was the plan, after all. The driver could still ram into them. But they wouldn't be going at such a high speed on the trail, and there'd be an ambush waiting for the thugs. Maybe they'd be able to capture at least one of them alive so they could get some answers.

"Everyone hold on," Jace said. "The turn is just ahead."

Lauren pulled in her breath and held it. There were wide ditches on each side of the trail, and if the SUV hit them again, they could land in one of those. They were filled with water and mud, and the cruiser would likely get stuck.

There was another thing that could go wrong, too. Simply put, the gunmen might not follow them. They might recognize this could be a trap and just speed away so they could regroup and come after them again.

Jace had to hit the brakes to slow down for the turn, but he was still going pretty fast when he took it. The trail was a mixture of gravel, dirt and grass, and judging from the way Jace had gripped the steering wheel, he must have expected them to go into another slide.

And they did.

The back of the cruiser fishtailed, slinging them around again, but Jace got them back on course. He didn't speed up right away, though, and Lauren knew why. He was waiting for the gunmen.

She lifted her head to look out the back window.

It seemed to take an eternity, but it was only a few seconds before she finally saw what she needed to see. The SUV made the turn, as well, and came after them. Jace hit the accelerator again.

"The reserve deputies and the Ranger should be about a half mile up," Jameson explained. He kept his eyes on the SUV but motioned for Lauren to get back down on the seat.

She did. But she hated she was being protected like this when all three of the men were high enough in the seats that they could be shot. Of course, the gunman's bullets would have to get through the glass first.

That thought had barely crossed her mind when there were more shots fired. These slammed into the trunk of the cruiser. Definitely not as "safe" as those on the roof since the trunk was right next to the backseat.

"What the hell?" Jace mumbled.

That put her heart right in her throat, and Lauren lifted her head again so she could see what'd caused his reaction. There was a motorcycle, and it was parked just beneath some trees just off the left side of the trail.

"Is that the Ranger?" Jace asked.

Jameson shook his head. "Maybe it's one of the reserve deputies. I'll ask Gabriel."

He took out his phone, no doubt to call their brother, but Jameson didn't get a chance to do that.

Because there was a blast.

It was deafening. Lauren couldn't be sure, but she thought maybe it'd come from the direction of the motorcycle. She was sure of something else, though. It hadn't been the sound of a bullet. No, this was something much, much bigger. And whatever it was, it hit them.

Hard.

Jace still had hold of the steering wheel, but it didn't seem to do any good. That was because whatever had hit them exploded into the front end of the cruiser. There were ditches here, too. Ones almost as wide as those on the road. And that was exactly where the blast sent them.

CAMERON DIDN'T KNOW what the guy by the motorcycle had shot at him. He'd barely had time to spot the man before he'd fired something. Not a grenade. The blast hadn't been big enough for that, but it'd been some kind of explosive device.

Jace cursed when the cruiser pitched to the left, and the deputy had no control when the tires on that side went into the ditch. Because of the rain, it was more of a small stream, and they instantly went into the bog.

Trapping them.

They were much too close to the motorcycle guy, since he was on the same side of the trail.

Cameron glanced down at Lauren to make sure she hadn't been hurt in the impact. She hadn't been, but she'd already pulled her gun and was about to sit up. He pushed her right back down.

Behind them, the SUV came to a stop. Not a fast one, either, which meant they'd slowed down enough, probably because the driver had known this was going to happen. And what had happened was the worst-case scenario for this plan. Because now they were trapped.

"I'll call the backup," Jameson said. He, too, still had his weapon drawn, and he was looking all around them.

Cameron was looking, too, but he could no longer see the man by the motorcycle. He'd likely slipped into the woods, and there were plenty of hiding places for him. The trees and underbrush were thick here.

"How far away is backup?" Lauren asked. She was shaking some, but not nearly as much as Cameron had expected her to be doing. Good. Because he might need her to help him shoot their way out of this.

He hated that she was in this position. Hated even more that he was the reason she was here. But Lauren and he were of a like mind on this. They'd wanted to do whatever it took to protect Patrick and Isaac.

And maybe that could still happen.

Cameron had to hold on to that hope. Unless the thugs had brought an army with them, then they might not be able to get to them in the cruiser. Added to that, backup was almost certainly on the way here, and they shouldn't be that far away.

"Backup's coming," Jameson verified when he finished his call.

Cameron looked back at the SUV again. No movement there. The men were staying inside. There was also no movement from anywhere in the woods, but he was dead certain more men were out there.

Hell.

"This could be a trap for the backup," Cameron told Jameson.

Jameson cursed, too, and made another call. Of course, backup would have anticipated that the thugs would be on the lookout for them, but they probably thought they'd be coming to a gunfight. There hadn't been a shot fired, though, since the blast that'd disabled them. That didn't mean, however, that more shots wouldn't come soon.

Cameron's phone rang, the sound knifing through the silence. Lauren gasped, and then she groaned when she saw *Unknown Caller* on the screen. It was almost certainly their attackers. Cameron answered and put it on speaker, but he didn't say a word.

"Deputy Doran," the caller said. "Looks like you and your woman are in a tight spot. I think this is what folks mean by sitting duck."

The thug was stating the obvious, but it still put a knot in Cameron's gut to hear it. "What do you want?" Cameron snapped, and he motioned to Jameson to play the recording on his phone. Within seconds, there was the sound of Isaac fussing.

"I want you and your woman, of course. Those kids, too," the thug said. "Good to know the little fellas weren't hurt during the blast."

"What if they had been?" Lauren snarled. "You could have hurt them. Is that what your boss wants you to do—hurt babies?"

There was plenty of anger in her voice, but Cameron figured it was also a stall tactic. The longer they kept him talking, the more time backup would have to arrive.

"Don't have a clue what my *boss* wants to do to them, and it falls under the heading of I don't care. I just want my money. And no, don't bother to start offering me a payoff. I'm more or less committed to this, you see."

Which meant he could be being blackmailed or coerced in some way. So Cameron tried a different angle. "If you want immunity, you've got it." That was a lie. As a deputy he couldn't make an offer like that unless he cleared it with the DA. "All you have to do is tell us who hired you."

"No more talk about that," the gunman growled. "Just shut up and listen." He sounded impatient now. Probably because he knew they would have already requested backup, and that time was running out for him. "You and your woman need to get out of the cop car."

"And the babies?" Cameron asked. "Which one

do we bring?" Because that would narrow down the identity of the person responsible for this. If the man said to bring Isaac, then it was either Duane or Julia. But Evelyn would want Patrick since he was her grandson.

"I would say just bring one of them, but since I don't know which one," the gunman snarled, "I'll be needing you to step out with both of them. And I'm not gonna do a countdown or anything. You come out with them now."

Cameron doubted the man would want to hear this, but he didn't have a choice. He couldn't take Lauren out there for her to be gunned down. "It's too risky for the babies."

"Hell, it's too risky for you!" the goon practically shouted. "Now, move. I'd better see that door opening right now."

Cameron looked at Jameson and Jace to see if they were ready for whatever was about to happen. They were. Jameson had turned off the recording, put his phone back in his pocket and he had a firm grip on his gun. So did Jace.

And Lauren.

"They'll come to the cruiser after us, won't they?" she asked.

As a minimum. And they didn't have to wait long for that minimum, either.

"Time's up," the gunman said, but the words had hardly left his mouth when Cameron saw something he didn't want to see. It was the guy who'd been by the motorcycle. This probably wasn't the one they'd been talking to since this man didn't have a phone.

However, he did have some kind of launcher.

And he aimed it at the cruiser.

Before Cameron could even react, another explosive came their way. It crashed into what was left of the front end of the cruiser, tearing the metal and engine apart. It also knocked out the front windshield. They had to shelter their eyes from the flying glass and debris.

"Still not convinced you should get out?" the goon on the phone said. "The next one goes right into the cop car where y'all are sitting."

It was a bluff. Possibly. But Cameron couldn't call him on that bluff, and he didn't have time to come up with a plan. They were going to have to run for it, and there was only one direction to go. To the right, away from the thug with the launcher. That meant they'd have to run directly in front of the SUV.

Cameron looked at Lauren, who'd just followed his gaze out the window. Judging from her expression she knew what was about to happen.

"Take both blankets, one in each arm," he instructed. That might save her from being gunned down.

Lauren gave a shaky nod and gathered them up. "When do we start running?" she asked.

"Now."

Cameron threw open the door and started shooting.

Chapter Sixteen

Lauren hadn't had nearly enough time to steel herself up for this, but maybe there was no chance of that happening anyway. Not with the strong possibility that they were all about to die.

Cameron got out ahead of her, took aim at the man by the motorcycle and sent several shots his way. Lauren didn't look back to see if that had pinned down the guy or sent him scrambling. She just ran as fast as she could while trying to keep hold of the blankets. Despite the rain and the slick, muddy surface, she raced across the narrow trail, went several yards into the woods and dropped behind a tree.

She had her gun. She was holding it in a death grip beneath the blankets. But no way did she have a clean shot. That was because Cameron, Jameson and Jace were in between the motorcycle thug and her.

"Run!" she called out to them.

They did, but they weren't hurrying as much as she'd done, and they were volleying their attention between the motorcycle and the SUV. Good thing, too, because it was only a handful of seconds before both SUV doors opened, and the armed men leaned out. They stayed in the SUV and behind the doors, using them for cover.

While they sent round after round of bullets at Cameron and the others.

Lauren didn't have a clean shot of them, either, so she could only pray that they reached safety.

Cameron and Jameson did. They ran toward her, but they only made it a few feet off the trail and ducked behind the first tree they reached. It was still much too close to the SUV, but at least they were no longer in a direct line of fire.

Unlike Jace.

He wasn't nearly as lucky.

Lauren watched in horror as a bullet slammed into Jace's arm.

She heard him make a sharp sound of pain, and he scurried to the front of the cruiser. It was a wreck, but at least he was out of the path of the men in the SUV. Not from the motorcycle guy, though, or anyone else who happened to be out here in these woods. That was why Lauren tried to keep watch for him.

Soon, very soon, Jace would need an ambulance, but there was little chance of getting one out here unless they stopped these hired guns. That meant killing them, since she figured they hadn't come out here with plans to surrender.

The thugs from the SUV continued to fire at Cameron and Jameson, forcing them to stay put, though

Cameron did look in her direction. Just a glimpse. And she saw the same worry on his face that was no doubt on hers.

She caught some movement from the corner of her eye. It wasn't by the motorcycle, where she'd last seen the guy with the launcher. It was a good fifteen feet past that. But it was the same man, all right. He was behind some dense shrubs, and he lifted something. Not a launcher this time. But rather a gun.

And he aimed it at Jace.

"Look out, Jace!" she yelled.

But Lauren did more than just shout out a warning. She dumped the blankets on the ground and shot at the guy. She missed. Cursed herself for doing that because the man dropped back out of sight. She had no doubt, though, that he was still there, waiting for a shot where he could finish off Jace.

Her phone dinged with a text message, and while Lauren hated to take her eyes off her surroundings, she knew this could be important. It was. It was from Cameron.

Stay put and keep holding the blankets, he texted. Backup can't get to us right away.

Lauren did pick up the blankets, but her breath froze. The fear wedged there in her throat that'd clamped shut.

No.

That wasn't what she'd wanted to hear.

They needed backup. Worse, it could mean the Ranger and reserve deputies had been hurt or killed.

Obviously, these hired guns had known they were trying to lead them to a trap. If they'd spotted the lawmen, then they could have taken them out before Jace had even driven onto the trail.

She forced herself to breathe. To think. Hard to do with the bullets still flying all around, not just from the SUV shooter but also from Cameron and Jameson.

Plus, she had to watch for the man with the launcher. He could send another one of those explosives at Jace. Or at Cameron and Jameson, for that matter. Lauren didn't think he would aim at her, though. Not as long as he thought she had the babies in her arms. It didn't make her feel better to know that she was safe while Cameron, Jace and her brother weren't.

Lauren adjusted her gun, holding it beneath the blankets, and she continued to keep watch. The gunman who'd had the launcher finally leaned out from cover again. Like before, he took aim at Jace. But this time, Jace must have seen him because he fired first. Unlike her shot, Jace's didn't miss, and the guy fell to the ground.

Good, one down and at least two to go.

It wasn't safe for Jace to try to make his way across the trail to her, but he did drop lower to the ground. She could see that he was grimacing in pain. However, he was also looking around to make sure there weren't others who could pick him off.

Even over the noise of the gunfire, Lauren heard another sound. A car engine. Someone was coming up the trail and would soon be behind the SUV. She hoped it was Gabriel or another cop, but she couldn't count on that. She had to do something to help.

Now that Jace was out of immediate danger, Lauren started moving. She stayed crouched as low as she could manage while still carrying the blankets, and she began to make her way to Cameron.

Jameson and he had almost certainly heard the car and knew that it could mean more trouble. If they had to fend off more gunmen, she wanted to be in a position to help.

Lauren kept moving. Kept checking her, too, to make sure Jace was all right. He was still in the same spot, and she didn't see any other hired thugs trying to get to him.

"Stay down," Cameron snapped when he spotted her. "Don't come any closer."

"I can help you return fire."

He didn't answer her, not with words, but he gave her a stern look while he continued to trade shots with the gunmen. Lauren did get down, but she went several more feet first and then took cover behind a tree. All in all, it wasn't a bad position because she had line of sight of Cameron and Jameson as well as Jace.

There was blood on his shirt.

The rain was soaking him, but the blood continued to flow. She saw him grimace again, and he pressed his hand over it. Probably to try to slow the bleeding.

In the distance she heard something else to let her know that things had gone wrong. More gunfire. It seemed to be coming from two areas—both up the trail and back by the road. The gunfire was probably why the backup couldn't get to them.

She kept her attention on their surroundings, but Lauren took out her phone again so she could try to text Gabriel. He almost certainly knew what was going on, but she wanted to make sure the babies were all right. Before she could press his number, though, her phone rang.

Unknown Caller.

Her heart thudded against her chest. Because the gunman was calling her. Maybe because Cameron was too busy shooting to answer. But it did make her wonder how he'd gotten her number.

She hit the answer button, but as Cameron had done earlier, Lauren didn't say anything. It didn't take long, though, before she heard the voice.

"Lauren," the caller said. "There's only one way for your brother and Cameron to get out of this alive. And that's for you to bring me the babies now."

CAMERON HAD HEARD Lauren's phone ring, and he'd hoped it was Gabriel calling to reassure her that he had a plan to rescue her. But after one look at her face, Cameron knew it wasn't that.

Something was wrong.

Of course, the worst possible scenario came to mind. That something bad had happened at the ranch; that they were under attack. There were plenty of people at Gabriel's to protect Patrick and Isaac, but that didn't mean one of the boys couldn't have been hurt.

He wasn't close enough to Lauren to hear what she was saying, but she was definitely responding to something the caller had said. Not a good response, either. Lauren cursed the caller, and then her gaze flew to him.

Yeah, something was definitely wrong, but he didn't think it was fear that he saw. Cameron thought she was angry. So angry that every visible muscle was tight.

Even though Cameron had insisted that she stay put, Lauren started toward him. She didn't exactly stay down, either. She hurried, but at least she was continuing to hold the blankets to her chest. Unfortunately, they no longer looked much like babies because the rain had soaked the blankets. It had soaked Lauren, too. The rain was dripping off her face.

When she was still several feet away, Cameron ran to her, pulling her behind the tree with Jameson and him. He was about to ask her what'd happened, but she just handed him the phone. Her hand was shaking. *She* was shaking. But her eyes were narrowed almost to slits.

"It's Julia," she said.

Cameron doubted the woman was calling to check on them or declare her innocence for the umpteenth time. No. She was the person behind this. Probably the person in the car that'd just come to a stop in back of the SUV.

Hell.

Of course, she was one of their main suspects, but it sickened him to think of this witch putting Lauren and everyone else in danger. And he figured Julia was doing that because she needed money. Now Cameron could feel his own surge of anger, and he hoped he got a chance to settle the score with this woman.

"What do you want?" Cameron snapped when he finally spoke to her. Jameson moved closer so he could hear over the drone of the rain.

"Lauren and Isaac," Julia said without hesitation. "Have them come to my car, and you, Patrick and anybody else you brought with you will be safe. You can even get an ambulance out here for your deputy friend."

Cameron wanted the ambulance for Jace, but that was too big of a price to pay. Jace would feel the same way about it, too.

"You really think I'll just allow Lauren and Isaac to go to you?" Cameron asked. "You'll kill them."

Now Julia hesitated. "No. I'm not about to kill my brother's son. Lauren and Isaac will be taken to an undisclosed location, and once I have the money from Alden's estate, I'll release them."

"Right." And he didn't bother to take the skepticism out of his voice.

Lauren was plenty skeptical, as well, and he didn't

think her trembling was all from the cold rain. It was also from the rage she was feeling right now. Cameron had to make sure that rage didn't cause Lauren to do something stupid. Like try to go after Julia.

"You don't believe me," Julia remarked. She sounded so calm she could have been discussing the weather, but Cameron figured the woman was also feeling loads of emotion. Fear being one of them. Julia had to know that so many things could go wrong now.

That applied to Lauren and him, as well.

"You should believe me," Julia went on. "I'll disappear after I have the money and settle my debts. I plan to move overseas. A place where I can't be extradited back here."

There were many countries that didn't have extradition treaties with the US, but Cameron still wasn't convinced.

"I figure you'll stay put, right here in Texas," Cameron said. "And you'll probably set up Duane or Evelyn to take the fall for this."

Silence. Which meant he was probably spot-on with his theory. No way would Julia take the blame for any of this.

"You need to hurry," Julia warned him, her voice crisp now. "Don't count on help from your lawmen friends, either, because my men are holding them off on the road."

Cameron didn't like the sound of that, and he hoped none of them had been hurt. The injury to

Jace was enough. "You've hired an awful lot of thugs for someone who's flat broke."

"Funded with money from Alden's company," she admitted. "And a little help from the person who loaned me money."

So the thugs belonged to the loan shark. That was why none of them had been willing to negotiate a deal with Cameron. Their boss wouldn't have killed them. And this way, the loan shark ensured that he'd get not only the money Julia owed him but then some, too. Heck, the loan shark might end up taking most of the entire estate. Along with killing Julia. But the woman probably hadn't realized that.

"Your deputy might have managed to take out the person who was manning the launcher," Julia went on. "But there's someone else out there who can do the same job. He has orders to fire if Lauren doesn't come to me with Isaac. You've got a minute to send her out here."

"I'll go," Lauren whispered.

Cameron cursed and muted the call. Even though Lauren already knew this, he thought it was worth repeating. "She wants you dead."

"Yes, but when I get to the car, she'll want to take a look at Isaac, to make sure I've brought the right baby. When she does that, I can escape."

There were way too many things that could go wrong—especially since Julia would have at least one hired gun in the car with her. Still, they didn't have a lot of options here. If the guy with the launcher fired at them, then they'd all die.

Cameron forced himself to think, and there was no completely safe way to handle this. But maybe he could do something to ensure that Lauren made it out of this alive.

"Make sure there's not another launcher," Cameron told Jameson.

Jameson nodded, and he started moving. Unlike Lauren had done, he kept low. Obviously trying to stay out of sight while he made his way closer to the cruiser and the area where they'd last seen the launcher.

"Give me thirty seconds before you start walking out to Julia," Cameron added to Lauren. "I'll try to get as close to Julia's car as possible so I can be in place to help you escape."

He gave one of the blankets an adjustment and gave her a quick kiss. Cameron wished there was time to say more. Exactly what, he didn't know. But he hated to think that these might be his last moments with her.

"Thirty seconds," he repeated, and Cameron started moving.

Thankfully, there was plenty of underbrush so he could keep hidden, but Julia had probably figured he'd be trying to do something exactly like this.

He counted off the seconds in his head, and once he was close to that thirty-second mark, Cameron stopped and got ready to fire. He considered just shooting into the windshield of Julia's car with the hopes he'd hit her or her goons. But then the guy with the launcher would no doubt retaliate.

Cameron felt the punch of dread go through him when Lauren stepped out. Right out in the open. Of course, that'd been the plan, but still, he hated that she had to be in harm's way like this.

"I'm coming," Lauren called out to Julia.

She had a bundled blanket in the crook of her right arm. And she also had her gun. It wasn't hidden nearly enough, but there was no way Cameron could warn her now. Lauren was walking directly to the car.

The car doors opened. Both on the driver's and front passenger's side, and even though no one got out, Cameron figured these were the hired goons. Julia was probably in the backseat, but he couldn't see her.

"You'll want to drop that gun," one of the thugs told Lauren.

Lauren stopped, hesitating, and she let go of it so that it fell to the ground. She started walking again. Only making it a few steps.

Before the shot blasted through the air.

LAUREN HEARD THE sound and braced herself for the bullet to hit her. The old saying was true. Her life did flash before her eyes. The pain and the happiness. She'd known that Cameron had been a big reason for a lot of her happiness, and she regretted that she had never told him that.

But the bullet didn't hit her.

Stunned, she stood there a moment before she realized the guy on the driver's side of Julia's car had fired the shot at Cameron. Lauren's stomach went to her knees, and she called out for him.

No response.

The anger came, quickly replacing the stunned fear, and Lauren charged toward the gunman.

"Don't shoot her," Julia yelled. "Not until we have the kid."

Lauren had figured all along that Julia had no plans to let her live, and Julia had just confirmed that. Since holding the baby gave Lauren some protection, she kept running. Except she didn't go to the driver. She ran to the other side of the vehicle, where she hoped to get her hands on Julia.

Behind her, she heard the explosion. Mercy, that was where Jameson had been going, and she prayed he hadn't been hurt. Maybe he'd managed to get out of the path before that blast went his way, but she couldn't risk even glancing over her shoulder to check on him.

There was another shot.

The bullet slammed into the driver, and it'd come from Cameron's direction. She prayed that meant he hadn't been hurt and added the same prayer for her brother.

The thug on the passenger's side took aim at Cameron, and he started shooting. One shot right after the other. And Cameron wasn't returning fire.

Lauren kept moving, pushing aside all the gunfire and the possibility that the gunman would turn his weapon on her. In case he tried that, she held the blanket even higher so that it would make it harder for her to kill him.

When Lauren reached the car, the thug stopped shooting at Cameron, and he reached out to grab her. She didn't give him a chance to do that, though. She used the entire weight of her body to ram into the car door, which, in turn, rammed into him. He cursed her and howled out in pain. But Lauren ignored him and threw open the back door.

Julia.

The woman sat there, alone on the backseat, and she had a gun aimed right at Lauren.

"Give me the kid," Julia snarled.

Her sister-in-law had never been friendly to her, but now Lauren saw the pure hatred in the woman's eyes. She was certain there was hatred in her own eyes, too. Hatred that she aimed at Julia.

Yelling at the top of her lungs, Lauren tossed the blanket at her. She caught just a glimpse of Julia's stunned look before Lauren launched herself at the woman. Pinpointing all of her rage into her fist, she punched Julia right in the face.

Julia didn't just sit there and take that, though. She let out her own feral yell, and she came at Lauren, grabbing her by the hair and shoving her back. They fell out of the car and onto the ground. Unfortunately, Julia landed on top of Lauren, and she whacked her gun across Lauren's jaw.

The pain slammed through Lauren so hard and nearly robbed her of her breath. Still, that didn't stop her from fighting back. Nor did the shots that she heard being fired all around them. Cameron and maybe Jameson were in a fight for their lives, but Lauren was in her own fight. One that she had to win so that she could help Cameron and the others.

Lauren managed to catch on to Julia's wrist to stop the woman from hitting her with the gun again, but Julia only punched her with her left hand. That one wasn't nearly as hard as the first one had been, but it still dazed her for a moment.

"You should have just brought the kid!" Julia shouted. "They'll kill me now, but first I'll make sure you're dead."

Lauren had no intention of just letting her do that. While she still had a grip on Julia's wrist, Lauren shoved up her hand—and Julia's gun slammed into the woman's chin. Julia cursed her again.

And pulled the trigger.

The gun was close to Lauren's ear. Too close. Because the blast from the bullet was so loud that it deafened her. But she had no trouble feeling, and even though Julia's shot had missed her, that didn't stop her from head-butting Lauren.

Enough of this. Lauren wasn't just going to lie there while Julia beat her into unconsciousness. Then she'd be an easy kill. She didn't intend to make any of this easy for Julia.

Lauren mustered as much energy as she could, and she threw Julia off her. She moved fast to pin the woman's hands to the ground by throwing her body over Julia's.

"Kill Cameron," Julia shouted out to her hired thug. "Kill him now." And the thug fired some shots.

That was not the right thing for Julia to say, and it caused a new wave of anger to wash through Lauren. She slammed her forearm into Julia's face, causing the woman's head to flop back. Lauren took full advantage of that. She ripped the gun from Julia's hand, turned toward the thug.

Lauren fired.

But her shot wasn't necessary. The thug was already in the process of falling to the ground. That was when she saw Cameron. Alive, thank God. And with his gun aimed right at the fallen man.

Beneath her, she felt Julia's body tense. The woman was probably about to gear up for another round of the fight. She didn't get a chance to do that, though. Cameron raced toward them, and he pointed his gun at Julia.

"Please move so I can shoot you," he said through clenched teeth.

Julia went limp, her hands dropping to her sides. Lauren didn't relax, though. She got up and took aim at the woman, as well.

Lauren risked a glance at Cameron to make sure

he was okay. He seemed to be. No blood anyway. She was certain she was bleeding, though, from the punches she'd taken from Julia.

The sound of running footsteps sent Cameron snapping in the direction of the cruiser. Lauren looked there, too, and saw a welcome sight.

Jameson.

Her brother seemed fine, too.

"The guy with the launcher's dead," Jameson said. "I don't see any other hired guns around, but we need to get out of here." He glanced down at Julia. "We can get that piece of slime behind bars."

Julia had a strange reaction to that. She looked up at Lauren and laughed. "It's not over," the woman said. "I had a backup plan in case something went wrong. In case you didn't bring the babies with you, after all."

"What do you mean?" Lauren asked, and she reminded herself that anything that came out of the woman's mouth could be a lie.

But this didn't feel like a lie.

Not with that sick smile on Julia's face.

"Evelyn didn't want any part of the violence," Julia continued. "She didn't want to get her hands dirty. But she's at the ranch now to get her grandson. And I sent enough hired guns with her to do just that."

Chapter Seventeen

Cameron couldn't get to his phone fast enough, and he prayed that Julia's threat was all just a bluff. But he also knew Evelyn. Knew that she was desperate to get her hands on Patrick, so she might indeed have fallen for something like this.

"Hurry," Lauren said. She was firing glances all around, no doubt looking for a way to get to the ranch ASAP.

"I'm calling Gabriel," he told her, and he pressed the number. It rang and then went to voice mail.

Hell.

That was not what Cameron wanted to hear. Apparently, neither did Lauren, because she hurried to Julia's car. "The keys are in the ignition."

If they took it they could leave immediately, especially since the cruiser had been disabled. "Jace..." Cameron mumbled.

"Go," Jameson insisted. "I'll stay with him and see if I can get the ambulance out here. If not, I can take the gunmen's SUV."

Cameron figured there were some concerns about the plan, but his bigger concern was getting to the boys. He ran to the car, motioning for Lauren to get in, but she had by the time he got behind the wheel.

There was no place to turn around, so he threw the car into Reverse. "Look for any kind of tracking devices," he added to Lauren.

He figured Julia wouldn't have put anything like that on the vehicle, but it was possible the loan shark had. That was just one possible obstacle. The next one was the hired guns that Julia said were at the end of the trail—the very place they needed to go to get back on the road to the ranch.

"I don't see anything," Lauren said. She shook her head, the panic in both her expression and her voice. "But if it's small enough, it could be hidden underneath something."

Yeah, and it probably wouldn't be that small. Still, it wasn't something he could worry about right now, especially since there was the biggest worry of all— possible gunmen at the ranch. And Gabriel was short some hands and deputies because they'd been at the sites where they were supposed to trap the gunmen.

They'd failed at that.

But Cameron couldn't fail at getting to Isaac and Patrick.

"Try calling Gabriel again," Cameron told her.

She did, all the while she was mumbling something. A prayer from the sound of it. Cameron said a few himself.

"Voice mail," Lauren relayed to him, and she groaned. Not an ordinary one but the kind that sounded as if she was about to cry.

"Keep trying," he pressed. "And get down on the seat."

He knew that was only going to cause her more alarm, but there was nothing he could do about it. They were approaching the end of the trail, and while he didn't hear any gunfire, that didn't mean the shooters weren't there. Added to that, the car probably wasn't bullet resistant like the cruiser.

While she kept redialing Gabriel's number, Lauren did sink lower in the seat, but she kept her head high enough to keep watch. Cameron was watching, too, and that was why he had no trouble spotting the three vehicles at the intersection of the trail and the road. One was a black SUV, identical to what the other hired guns had driven. There was also a cruiser and a truck that he knew belonged to one of the ranch hands.

"I don't see any gunmen," Lauren said on a rise of breath.

Other than Allen, the ranch hand, neither did he. He had the butt of a rifle resting against his hip. There was a Texas Ranger next to him and a reserve deputy on the other side of the trail. Cameron slowed down and lowered his window.

"The gunmen are dead," Allen said to Cameron. He tipped his head to the trail. "How about up there?"

"Dead. There could be trouble at the ranch. Lauren and I are headed there now, but you should go check on Jameson and Jace. Jace will need an ambulance. Is the road clear?" he asked without pausing.

"As far as I know. I'll follow you," Allen volunteered.

Cameron thanked him but didn't wait for the man. He backed out onto the road, and now that there was room to turn around, that was exactly what he did. Fast. And he sped toward the ranch.

The rain had slowed some, but there was still plenty of water on the road. It was a risk, but Cameron didn't slow down. Everything inside him was yelling for him to get to the boys as fast as he could.

"Gabriel," Lauren said.

Finally. But Cameron didn't breathe easier just yet. "Put the call on speaker. Are the boys okay?" Cameron asked the moment Lauren did that. "Julia said there could be gunmen at the ranch."

"Yeah to both. The boys are fine, but we've definitely got some armed thugs."

The panic slammed through Cameron. Through Lauren, too, because he heard her make a hoarse sob.

"That's why I couldn't answer your call," Gabriel continued. "I'm out by the barn where I just took out two of them."

Two. But Cameron was betting there were more than that. Heck, Julia could have sent a dozen of them.

"Julia sent them," Cameron explained. "And Evelyn will be with them."

"We have Evelyn in handcuffs, facedown on the porch, but we haven't managed to round up a final gunman yet. He's somewhere near the front of the ranch. Maybe by the road. If I thought it would do any good, I'd tell you two to wait until—"

"We'll be there in about a minute," Cameron interrupted.

"I figured you'd say that. Just be careful because this guy has a rifle with a scope." Gabriel ended the call, probably because he had his hands full making sure the house was safe. Which was exactly what Cameron wanted him to do.

"I'm not staying down on the seat this time," Lauren said. "I want to stop this guy."

Like Gabriel, Cameron knew he didn't stand a chance of winning that argument with her. Besides, he might need her. Lauren had proven herself to be a good shot, and he wanted all the backup he could get. No way did he want this guy firing anywhere near Gabriel's house.

Cameron slowed when they approached the turn for the ranch, and he drew his gun, keeping it in his hand, but he didn't see anyone. Well, no one that he didn't recognize anyway. There were two ranch hands, both armed, and they were in a truck parked on the side of the road. He pulled to a stop next to them and lowered his window again.

"We lost sight of the guy," the hand said. "But he came this way, and he's wearing all black."

That wasn't an especially good camouflage color,

but he could be hiding in the trees that were nearby. Of course, that would be the first place someone would look for him. And maybe this man knew that.

"Check the ditch on your side," Cameron told Lauren.

He kept his window down and moved the car up so the hands' truck wouldn't be obstructing his view. He angled his head to get a better look. Like the ditches on the trail, these were filled with water. Water that was almost black under the iron-gray sky and rain.

Cameron crept along at a snail's pace, searching, while Lauren did the same on the other side. He was a good twenty yards from the ranch hands before he spotted something.

The gunman.

The guy was squatting chest-deep in the water. And yes, he had a rifle. One that he immediately started turning toward Cameron.

Cameron didn't even bother telling Lauren to watch out. There wasn't time. He just took aim and fired. Not one shot but three. The bullets slammed into the guy's chest, and they must have killed him instantly because the thug didn't even get the chance to pull the trigger.

Lauren sat there, frozen for a moment. She'd seen way too much death in the past couple of days, but she didn't leave her attention on the dead gunman for long. She looked at Gabriel's house. She didn't need to tell Cameron to hurry there now. He did. Because they both had to see for themselves that the boys were truly okay.

"Cameron shot the gunman," she said to Gabriel when she called him. "Yes, he's dead. Was anyone hurt at the ranch?"

Since she hadn't put this call on speaker and because his heartbeat was drumming in his ears, Cameron didn't hear what Gabriel said. However, the news must have been good because Lauren released the breath she'd been holding.

"No one's hurt," she relayed to Cameron when she ended the call.

Cameron was glad for that, but he wasn't feeling any relief yet and wouldn't until they were inside.

He went too fast again, the tires shimmying over the slick surface, but he managed to get them to Gabriel's. Before he'd even brought the car to a full stop, Lauren was out and running to the porch. Cameron was right behind her. There was no sign of Evelyn, thank goodness.

When Cameron went through the front door, he expected Lauren to already be on her way to the bathroom or wherever they'd moved the boys. But she wasn't. She was in the foyer with Jodi.

"Where's Evelyn?" Cameron asked, hoping the woman wasn't in the house.

"One of the Rangers took her into town to lock her up," Jodi answered. "I'm thinking this will pretty much put an end to any challenge she might have for custody."

Yes, it would. That was the silver lining in this. The other silver lining was Lauren.

Lauren whirled around to Cameron when he shut the door, and before he even saw it coming, she was in his arms. She kissed him. Not one of those passion-laced kisses that'd led to sex. This one seemed to be from pure relief.

"You saved my life," she said, her voice cracking.

There were tears in her eyes. And bruises and small cuts on her face from where Julia had punched her. It made him want to go back and throttle the woman. But Cameron didn't want to give Julia another moment of his time.

"And you saved mine," he answered.

Lauren nodded, managed a half smile and brushed another kiss on his mouth. "Good. Because I'm in love with you. Now, wipe the blood off your chin so we can see Isaac and Patrick."

He automatically reached to take care of the blood, but then her words sank in. It was too late, though, for him to respond because Lauren took off running toward the hall bathroom.

Jodi just shrugged. "I think the only person surprised by that I-love-you is *you*."

What? Cameron shook his head. That certainly wasn't common knowledge.

Was it?

Again, there was no time to dwell on it because he hurried after Lauren. And he found her, all right. She was on the bathroom floor and had both boys in her arms. She was showering them with kisses. Isaac liked it because he was giggling, but Patrick was fussing and trying to get away from her so he could get to his toy horse.

Cameron scooped up both the boy and the horse in his arms, and Patrick rewarded him with a sloppy kiss on the cheek. That kiss went a long way to soothing the adrenaline that was still surging through him.

"Is it okay for us to leave the bathroom?" Merilee asked. "Because it seems as if Lauren and you should have some family time with the boys." Dara added a sound of agreement.

Family time. That made it sound as if their marriage—a real marriage—was a done deal.

Cameron nodded. "Just stay inside and don't go near any windows," Cameron instructed. He needed to go out and check on Gabriel, to make sure the danger had passed before things could start getting back to normal.

Well, his new normal anyway. Whatever that would be.

He sank down on the floor next to Lauren, and Patrick and Isaac must have taken that as playtime because both boys went to the stash of toys that was all over the bathroom floor and started bringing them to Lauren and him.

Lauren turned to Cameron, and she eked out another smile. "Everything considered, you don't look shell-shocked."

Then he was covering it well, because he was.

Shell-shocked about the attack, about how close they'd come to dying and Julia's obsessive greed. But what Lauren had told him was at the top of that list of surprising things.

I'm in love with you.

Cameron was about to ask her if it was true, but she leaned in, and with that smile still in place she kissed him. It wasn't a relief kiss this time. No, this one had some heat to it. When she finally broke away, his breath was a little thin, but he was ready to launch into the conversation they needed to have.

But the footsteps stopped him.

Since the boys were right there, Cameron drew his gun and pivoted in the direction of the doorway. However, it wasn't a gunman. It was Gabriel. He glanced at all of them before his attention settled on his sister.

"Are you okay?" he asked.

Lauren nodded. She touched a bruise on her cheek that had obviously gotten Gabriel's attention. "Trust me, Julia looks worse. I got in some punches, too."

Gabriel winced a little, probably because he hated having to hear about his kid sister being in a fistfight with a would-be killer. It would certainly give Cameron some nightmares for years to come. They'd gotten damn lucky that Julia's shot had missed.

"Jameson has Julia on the way to jail," Gabriel continued. "And I think we got all the hired guns, not just here at the ranch but also the ones on the trails,"

Gabriel added to Cameron. "But everyone should stay in for a while until we've searched the grounds."

Good. Cameron didn't want to take any more risks with Lauren or the babies. "Has Julia said anything else?"

Gabriel shook his head. "She just yammered about wanting her lawyer. She'll want a plea deal but won't get one. I'll make sure of that. And we have enough from what Julia said to arrest the loan shark."

"That would hopefully keep the guy off the streets for the rest of his life. After all, he'd supplied the hired guns who'd killed Maria."

Lauren shook her head. "I still don't know why Julia sent those men to my house. She knew about the swap so why didn't she just try to take Isaac?"

"Because I think she wanted concrete proof of the swap," Gabriel answered. "If she'd managed to get you out of the picture, she would want to be able to prove that she had Alden's son in her custody."

True, but Cameron seriously doubted Julia would have kept Isaac around any longer than necessary. Only until she'd gotten her hands on the money.

Gabriel hitched his thumb to the front of the house. "I need to go out and check on the hands."

"I can help," Cameron volunteered.

"No," Gabriel said without hesitation. "You should stay here and work things out with Lauren." He paused and lifted an eyebrow when Cameron just stared at him. "Jodi mentioned what she'd heard in the foyer."

Great. Now Gabriel might want to punch him. Except he didn't make any move to do that. However, Gabriel did glare at him some.

"Just make Lauren happy," Gabriel growled. "Because if you don't, you'll have to answer to me."

Lauren huffed. "Let Cameron get his footing first before you go all alpha on him." Then she added a wink to her brother.

It seemed, well, such a light moment, considering they were only minutes out of an attack. But then it was hard to stay gloom and doom with the boys crawling all over them. Even Gabriel was smiling when he strolled away.

"My footing?" Cameron asked.

"Yes. I figured you'd need some time to come to terms with me telling you I love you."

He opened his mouth, closed it and tried to come up with a good answer to that. "You meant it?"

Her eyebrow came up. "Of course I did. You thought it was some heat of the moment thing?"

"I didn't know," he admitted. "I thought maybe you said that because of the boys."

She didn't say, "What?" but that expression was all over her face.

"You know, because you want us to have a life together with the boys," he clarified. And he was obviously not gaining any ground here. She was frowning now.

Lauren huffed again, slipped her hand around the back of his neck and kissed him. Really kissed him.

This one had much too high of a heat level considering they weren't alone.

"Do you know now?" She kept her mouth right next to his as if ready to convince him again.

Cameron didn't need convincing, but he kissed her anyway. There it was. More than the heat. More than this insane attraction that had been brewing for years. It was deeper than that, and now Cameron could finally tell her.

"I love you," he said, taking Lauren into his arms. "Not because of the boys, either—though they're a sweet bonus. I love you because of us. Because of you and me."

That was the right thing to say because Lauren smiled and pulled him to her for another kiss.

* * * * *

Look for the next book in
USA TODAY *bestselling author Delores Fossen's*
BLUE RIVER RANCH *miniseries,*
ROUGHSHOD JUSTICE,
available next month.

And don't miss the previous titles in the
BLUE RIVER RANCH *series:*

ALWAYS A LAWMAN
GUNFIRE ON THE RANCH

Available now from Harlequin Intrigue!

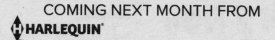

SPECIAL EXCERPT FROM

A killer stole her voice. Now she's ready to take it back.
Don't miss the next chilling installment in the
SHADES OF DEATH *series*
from USA TODAY *bestselling author Debra Webb.*

Turn the page for a sneak peek from
THE LONGEST SILENCE
by **Debra Webb**, *coming March 2018.*

New York Times *bestselling author Sandra Brown*
calls it "a gripping read."

The phone wouldn't stop ringing. The annoying sound echoed off the dingy walls of the tiny one-room apartment.

Joanna Guthrie chewed her thumbnail as she stared at the damned cell phone. Three people had this number: her boss, a research analyst she occasionally worked with and Ellen. If it was work, the caller would simply leave a message, but it wasn't work—it was Ellen.

Jo's foot started to tap so she stood and paced the floor. "Not answering."

Why should she answer? The calls came about three or four times a year and they were always the same. Ellen would complain about her life and her husband and her kids. She would bemoan the hand fate had dealt her. She would never be whole. Nothing she attempted fixed her. Not the shrinks or the meditation or the yoga or any of the other crazier shit she'd tried, like cocaine, and certainly not the alcohol.

The ringing stopped.

Jo stared at the phone. Two minutes tops and it would start that fucking ringing again. She closed her eyes and exhaled a measure of the frustration always generated by calls from Ellen. Guilt immediately took its place. No matter the reason, whenever Ellen called Jo always wound up feeling guilty whether she answered the damned phone or not. A voice mail carried the same guilt-generating effect.

"Not my fault." She paced the room like a freshly incarcerated criminal on the front end of a life sentence.

Ellen had chosen her own path. She'd made the decision to pretend to be normal. Dared to marry and to have children. Jo shook her head. How the hell could she do that after what they'd gone through—what they'd done? Now the woman spent every minute of every day terrified that she would somehow disappoint her family or that something bad would happen to them because of her. Or, worse, that someone would discover her secret—their secret.

MDWEXP1017

Deep breath. "Not my problem."

Jo had made the smarter choice. She'd cut ties with her family and friends. No boyfriends, much less husbands. No kids for damned sure. If she wanted sexual release she either took care of it herself or she picked up a soldier from one of the clubs in Killeen. She didn't go to church; she didn't live in the same town for more than a year. She never shared her history with anyone. Not that there was anything in her past that would give anyone reason to suspect the truth, but she hated the looks of sympathy, the questions.

The past was over and done. Dragging it into the present would not change what was done.

She had boundaries. Boundaries to protect herself. She never wasted time making small talk, much less friends. Besides, she wasn't in one place long enough for anyone to notice or to care. Since her employer was an online newspaper, she rarely had to interact face-to-face with anyone. In fact, she and the boss had never met in person and he was the closest thing to a friend she had.

Whatever that made her, Jo didn't care.

Hysterical laughter bubbled into her throat. Even the IRS didn't have her address. She used the newspaper's address for anything permanent. Her boss faxed her whatever official-looking mail she received, and then shredded it. He never asked why. Jo supposed he understood somehow.

She recognized her behavior for what it was—paranoia. Plain and simple. Six years back she'd noticed one of those health fairs in the town where she'd lived. Probably not the most scientific or advanced technology since it was held in a school cafeteria. Still, she'd been desperate to ensure nothing had been implanted in her body—like some sort of tracking device—so she'd scraped up enough money to pay for a full-body scan. Actually, she'd been short fifty bucks but the tech had accepted a quick fuck in exchange. After all that trouble he'd found nothing. Ultimately that was a good thing but it had pissed her off at the time.

A ring vibrated the air in the room.

Enough. Jo snatched up the phone. "What do you want, Ellen?"

The silence on the other end sent a surge of oily black uncertainty snaking around her heart. When she would have ended the call, words tumbled across the dead air.

"This is Ellen's husband."

A new level of doubt nudged at Jo. "Art?"

She had no idea how she'd remembered the man's name. Personal details were something else she had obliterated from her life. Distance and anonymity were her only real friends now.

Now? She almost laughed out loud at her vast understatement. Eighteen years. She'd left any semblance of a normal life behind eighteen years ago. Jesus Christ, had it only been eighteen?

Don't miss
THE LONGEST SILENCE,
available March 2018 wherever
MIRA® Books and ebooks are sold.

www.Harlequin.com

Rachel slipped her arms around his neck and kissed him back. Not shy or reluctant, it was a bold, hungry kiss that set him on fire. He swayed against her, drunk on the thrill of her lips on his, their tongues tangling, their breaths mingling.

Seconds later, she pulled away and placed an open hand against his chest, gently pushing him away. He was crazy with wanting her and was certain she could feel the pounding of his heart.

"See you tomorrow," she whispered as she opened the door and slipped back inside the house.

Tomorrow couldn't come too soon.

Dawn was lighting the sky before Rachel gave up on the tossing and turning and any chance of sound sleep. Her life was spinning out of control at a dizzying pace.

Two days ago, she'd had a career. She'd known what she would be doing from day to day. Admittedly, she'd still been struggling to move past the torture Roy Sales had put her through, but she was making progress.

Two days ago, she wasn't making headlines, another major detriment to defending Hayden. The terrors she was trying so hard to escape would be front and center.

People would stare. People would ask questions. Gossip magazines would feed on her trauma again.

Two days ago she hadn't met Luke Dawkins. Her stomach hadn't fluttered at his incidental touch. There had been no heated zings of attraction when a rugged, hard-bodied stranger spoke her name or met her gaze.

A kiss hadn't rocked her with desire and left her aching for more. She put her fingertips to her lips, and a craving for his mouth on hers burned inside her.

This was absolutely crazy.

She kicked off the covers, crawled out of bed, padded to the window and opened the blinds. The crescent moon floated behind a gray cloud. The universe held steady, day following night, season following season, the earth remaining on its axis century after century.

She didn't expect that kind of order in her life, but neither could she continue to let the demonic Roy Sales pull the strings and control her reactions.

She had to fight to get what she wanted—once she decided what that was. She'd spend the next two or maybe three days here in Winding Creek trying to figure it all out. Then she'd drive back to Houston and face Eric Fitch Sr. straight on.

There were no decisions to make about Luke Dawkins. Once he learned of her past, he'd see her through different eyes. And he'd definitely learn about her past, since she was making news again. He'd pity her, and then he'd move on.

Who could blame him? Her emotional baggage was killing her.

*Don't miss
DROPPING THE HAMMER by Joanna Wayne,
available April 2018 wherever
Harlequin Intrigue® books and ebooks are sold.*

www.Harlequin.com

THE WORLD IS BETTER WITH

Romance

Harlequin has everything from contemporary, passionate and heartwarming to suspenseful and inspirational stories.

Whatever your mood, we have a romance just for you!

Connect with us to find your next great read, special offers and more.